GIRLS
ON
THE
VERGE

GIRLS
ON
THE
VERGE

HENRY HOLT AND COMPANY · NEW YORK

Henry Holt and Company, *Publishers since 1866*
Henry Holt® is a registered trademark of Macmillan Publishing Group, LLC
175 Fifth Avenue, New York, New York 10010 • fiercereads.com

Library of Congress Cataloging-in-Publication Data
Names: Waller, Sharon Biggs, 1966– author.
Title: Girls on the verge / Sharon Biggs Waller.
Description: First edition. | New York : Henry Holt and Company, 2019. | Summary:
    Camille, seventeen, gives up her spot at a prestigious theater camp to drive from Texas
    to New Mexico to get an abortion, accompanied by her friends Annabelle and Bea.
Identifiers: LCCN 2018015681 | ISBN 9781250151698 (hardcover)
Subjects: | CYAC: Coming of age—Fiction. | Abortion—Fiction. | Best friends—Fiction. |
    Friendship—Fiction. | Actors and actresses—Fiction. | Autombile travel—Fiction. |
    Texas—Fiction.
Classification: LCC PZ7.W15917 Gir 2019 | DDC [Fic]—dc23
LC record available at https://lccn.loc.gov/2018015681

Our books may be purchased in bulk for promotional, educational, or business use. Please
contact your local bookseller or the Macmillan Corporate and Premium Sales Department at
(800) 221-7945 ext. 5442 or by email at MacmillanSpecialMarkets@macmillan.com.

First edition, 2019 / Designed by Katie Klimowicz
Printed in the United States of America
10 9 8 7 6 5 4 3 2 1

For my niece and best friend, Ashley,
and for my aunt Pam, who inspired me to join
the fight when I was a little girl—
we are three generations of feminists

No woman can call herself free who does not own and control her body. No woman can call herself free until she can choose consciously whether she will or will not be a mother.

—Margaret Sanger

JUNE 25, 2013

Texas State Senator Wendy Davis (D) stands in her pink sneakers holding a thirteen-hour filibuster to block Senate Bill 5, which restricts abortion access in the state. The bill bans abortions after twenty weeks, requires clinics to meet the same requirements as surgical centers, requires the clinics' doctors to have hospital admitting privileges, and requires a revisit to the doctor fourteen days after a medical abortion. She succeeds.

JULY 16, 2013

At the end of June, Texas Governor Rick Perry calls a special session to vote on House Bill 2 (HB2), which would set forth provisions that would result in closing the majority of abortion clinics in the state of Texas. The bill is signed into law on July 18.

JUNE 2014

As of this date, only nineteen abortion clinics remain open for the entire 269,000 square miles that make up Texas, populated by more than five million women of reproductive age.

ONE

JUNE 30

I've been ready to leave for the past hour, but that doesn't mean I want to. I didn't sleep. I lay in bed all night, watching the glowing red numbers on my alarm clock blink down the hours.

I straighten the quilt my grandma gave me for what seems like the hundredth time.

My phone buzzes, startling me.

Here. I'm early so take your time.

I pick up my backpack and purse and take a last look around my room to make sure I have everything.

I shut my door and head down the stairs, sliding my hand along the banister worn smooth from seventeen years' worth of touching. I make sure to avoid the squeaky step Dad always promises to fix but never will.

In the kitchen, I get a glass of water and gulp it down. The refrigerator hums, the hall clock ticks, the AC makes that weird noise that no electrician can figure out. It's strange the things you notice when you're really paying attention. The family pictures on the dining room wall across from me have hung there my whole life. There's a formal portrait of my grandma and mom, both of them in powder blue dresses, standing side by side. Next to it, a collage of my brother and me from kindergarten to junior year, baby-toothed smiles to awkward braces, a blank space reserved for my senior picture. And then there's my parents on their wedding day. Dad in his rented tux, Mom in her glittery gown and poofy veil. She holds a huge bouquet of lilies.

I scribble a note for my parents, draw a heart on it, and pin it to the bulletin board. I throw a couple of bananas, two granola bars, and a bottle of Sprite into a plastic bag, cram my feet into my Chucks, and open the door.

The sun is just starting to come up, but it's already hot. The paperboy appears over the hill; his loaded bag, crossed over his chest, pulls him sideways. I stop and watch as he flings the folded newspapers at the houses. They all fall short, landing on lawns. But the next one thunks onto my neighbor's porch, and the boy pumps his fist in the air.

Annabelle, seeing me, jumps out of the car and opens the passenger door.

Annabelle's car seats are covered with black fleece seat covers embroidered with the words *Black Cherry* over the headrests. A cobalt-blue evil eye swings from her rearview mirror by a leather strap. The floor is littered with flattened foam coffee cups. I carefully place my feet between a Giddyup cup and a Sonic one.

Annabelle has two orange plastic go-cups of coffee in her cup holders. The smell of the coffee makes me feel nauseous and hungry at the same time. She gets in the driver's side and shuts her door. "Sorry the car is such a mess. I didn't have time to shovel her out." She points to the cups of coffee. "I did bring nectar of the gods, though. And I wore my new favorite T-shirt."

I look at it. I STAND WITH WENDY DAVIS, it reads. And underneath the caption is a pair of pink sneakers.

"I thought we could use some of Wendy's courage. Coffee and courage, what more do we need?" She pauses for a moment, studying me. "Are you okay?"

I shake my head. "No, not really."

"We don't have to do this if you don't want to," Annabelle says. "We can turn around at any point. Just say the word."

"I do," I blurt out, a little harder than I mean to. "I mean . . . I do want to do this."

"It's going to be all right, Camille."

Annabelle grabs one of the coffees from the cup holder, takes a sip, puts her car in gear, and drives off.

"Didn't you have a Bug before? I remember you driving a yellow Volkswagen," I say.

"I sold her before I went to England. I bought Buzzi for when I'm home."

"Buzzi?"

"That's what I named this car—after Ruth Buzzi. Have you heard of her?"

I shake my head.

"She's this comedian from the sixties. She lives near Stephenville on this big horse ranch, and she collects all these cool vintage cars with her husband. She used to be on *Sesame Street* a lot. Anyway, I'd love to have vintage cars like hers someday." Annabelle pats the steering wheel. "Buzzi's not much of a car, but she tries."

"I've never heard of anyone naming a car before."

"You gotta name your car! It's the only way to really get to know it. Otherwise it's just a hunk of metal and wheels." She smiles and pushes the gearshift.

Annabelle looks so cool shifting, like she's a race car driver. After she shifts, she leaves her hand on the gear knob, her fingers cupping the bottom of it. I like how that looks. Kind of tough. Like you really know what you're doing and don't really care what anyone thinks about it.

"Is it hard to drive a stick shift?"

"It is at first. But then it's easy when you get the hang of it. My cousin taught me because my asshat of a father couldn't be bothered to."

I reach for a granola bar to settle my stomach. I eat it, watching out the window as the familiar landmarks of my town go by: the Holler Up, Jess's Jewelers, the Giddyup.

"God, I'm so glad to get out of Johnson Creek," Annabelle says.

"Even if it's a shitty reason why," I say. My shoulders are so tense, my muscles ache.

"So, listen. Bea called me last night."

"What? God, she never gives up." I should have known that Bea would search for a work-around. "Did she try to talk you out of taking me?"

"No. She wants to come."

"Well, she can't."

I take a sip of coffee, but the taste of it makes me feel pukey. I jam the cup back into the cup holder and grab the plastic bag. I dump the contents on the back seat and put the bag on my lap, just in case. I open the Sprite and take a sip.

"Do you need me to pull over?" Annabelle asks, casting a nervous look my way. "I mean, I won't hate you if you puke, but I'd rather you not."

"No. I'm okay."

"I told her I'd ask you, but I wouldn't guarantee it."

"I don't know why she'd want to."

"She told me she wants to support you."

We reach the YMCA. A pack of boys are running laps around the track outside. We stop at a traffic light by the chain-link fence that borders the track. As the pack gets closer, I can see their arm muscles flexing as they run. Their eyes are intense, and their shirts are soaked with sweat.

Guys get to run in the fresh air and then probably hang out with their girlfriends or their buddies while I get to travel to nearly Mexico to chase down some pills.

Annabelle takes a drink from her coffee and looks at the runners over her go-cup. "I can't imagine running around a track at the butt-crack of dawn like that."

"Me either."

Annabelle rolls the window down and sticks her head out. "Hey, assholes!" she yells. One of the boys in the back of the pack turns his head.

I can't help it. I burst out laughing.

She looks over at me and grins. "So, what do you want to do?"

If I say no to Bea after she has tried to reach out, I'm pretty much ending our friendship. I can't stand the thought of that. But I also can't stand the thought of listening to her trying to convince me to change my mind. I sigh. "She can come."

I direct Annabelle to Bea's house. She's waiting on the porch step already. A huge duffel bag, a pillow, and a grocery bag rest at her feet. "Overpacked as usual," I mutter.

Bea gets up and walks toward the car. Mrs. Delgado waves at us from the door. It's just after seven o'clock, yet she's already fully dressed in white pants and a striped shirt and pearls. Her hair is gathered into a bun.

Annabelle gets out and goes up the walk to help Bea. I stay in the car, staring straight ahead. The driver's door opens, and Bea climbs into the back.

I don't turn around. I don't look at her. "You say one thing to try to make me change my mind, Beatrice Delgado, and I swear we'll dump you on the side of the road."

"I know," Bea says. She puts her hand on the seat by my shoulder. "I promise I won't."

6

Annabelle slides in, puts on her seat belt, and drives off.

"Why do you want to come anyway?" I ask.

She takes her hand away. "You're my best friend, and I should be here with you."

It's hard to believe that just ten days ago, my life was exactly what I wanted it to be. I was heading to Willow, a supercompetitive theater camp, and I'd played my dream role of Ophelia at the midsummer production of *Hamlet* at the Globe Southwest Youth Theater. The actor who played Hamlet—a very dreamy boy from France—liked me. And that very same boy, Léo, was going to be at said camp sans parental supervision for a whole week.

I stare out the window and hope no one sees the tears in my eyes.

TWO
JUNE 21

I feel a tap on my shoulder.

"Do you want to dance?"

I turn around and Léo is there, all six feet of gorgeousness, and I swear I swoon in French.

"I am dancing," I say, even though I'm standing dead still.

He makes a face. "Well, that is very sad because I was hoping you would dance with me."

"I don't want to make you sad."

An old song from the eighties starts to play, "Time After Time."

If you fall I will catch you—I'll be waiting. Time after time . . .

He steps toward me and puts his hands on my waist, and I set mine on his shoulders. I don't know how kids dance in his country. I hope he doesn't start waltzing or something. But we do the ubiquitous high school slow dance, shuffling around in a circle, swaying back and forth. Bea, dancing with Mateo, gives me a look that says *I told you so*. The song ends, and I remove my hands from Léo's shoulders, even though I *really* don't want to stop touching him.

"Do you want to go outside?" Léo asks.

I would go anywhere with you, I nearly blurt out, but I catch myself. "Sure," I say as casually as I can. Léo takes my hand and leads me through the crowd. I've held hands onstage with him tons of times, but this is not the same thing. I like the way he holds my hand—palm to palm, instead of threading his fingers through mine.

"I hate closing night," I say. "I hate saying goodbye to my character."

"Me too," he says. He casts a glance at me, shy, or maybe uncertain. "I am very glad you are going to Willow."

"I'm glad you're going to Willow, too." I wonder how long he'll hold my hand or whether I should drop it or let him decide.

We're a little way from the theater when he stops. "I like your hair like this," he says, gently tugging my braid.

"It's Ophelia's hair," I say. "I only borrowed it."

"I'm sure she doesn't mind lending it to you."

"No, I don't think she's rolling over in her grave."

"And this flower thing you're wearing. You smell like a pixie."

"That's some line. You've smelled a pixie before?" I say.

"Of course," he says. "Hasn't everyone?"

"Not that I know of," I say, laughing. "It must be a French thing."

He shrugs. "Perhaps."

We stand there for a moment, and I try to find something else to say. "Um, do you want to see the creek?" I ask.

He taps his finger on his chin, pretending to think. "A 'creek'?"

"It's like a stream. Or a brook. A small river."

"Ah, *oui. Un ruisseau.* I would like to see a creek, yes."

He follows me down the path. The creek runs behind the theater, bordered by a band of woods. There's a steep path, and I've never seen anyone but me there.

The path opens up down a little hill and to the edge of the creek. The wind is waving the tree branches around, and the creek rushes over a bundle of sticks and logs jammed against the side of the bank, making that babbling noise that everyone loves. Air from the day mixed with air from the night creates weird pockets of warm and cool.

"Camille! *C'est très formidable*," Léo says, looking around. "It's like Ophelia's water, where she drowned herself."

I like how Léo says my name. His accent makes it sound romantic. Special. His face glows in the moonlight.

We sit on a patch of grass on the bank. A cool breeze cuts through the cotton of my dress, and I nudge a little closer to Léo.

"Where do you live in France?" I ask.

"I live in the Dordogne, way in the southwest of France. There we have troglodyte dwellings and cave paintings and a cathedral where the stone steps are worn in the middle from pilgrims climbing on their knees."

"That sounds painful," I say. "Have you climbed the stairs on your knees?"

"No. Only on my feet."

"What's a troglodyte dwelling?"

"A place where troglodytes dwell."

I shove him, and he falls backward onto the bank and rolls into a ball, pretend-moaning in pain.

I pull up some grass and fling a handful at him. "Seriously, what is it?"

He sits up and runs his hands through his hair, making it stand up. He laughs. "I told you already."

I clap the dirt off my hands and take my phone out of my dress pocket. "It sounds like you don't know, so I'll just google it." I go to nudge Léo with my shoulder, but he's turning toward me and I end up against his chest. I stay there, like it's perfectly normal, and start searching online for troglodyte dwellings.

He puts his hand over my phone. "I'll tell you. These are houses that are built into the front of caves." Léo drapes his arm around my shoulders. Everywhere his arm touches feels like a kiss. He holds me close. I can hear his breath, feel his chest rise and fall under my cheek, hear the thump of his heart. I wonder if this is what falling in love feels like—comfort, safety, excitement, and desire for that one person, all bunched up together.

"Tell me a story about your home," I say.

Léo thinks for a moment. "I'll tell you about a cave in the Vézère valley called Grotte de Rouffignac."

"Okay, tell me about the Grotte de, uh, what you said."

"You go in a little electric train. At the beginning of the cave you see hollows of clay big enough for an elephant, but these are dens of cave bears."

11

"Cave bears? That sounds made up."

"And then there are pictures of mammoths drawn into the clay walls with fingers, and handprints pressed into the wall over thirteen thousand years ago. The train goes, and the dark takes over so you can't even see your hand in front of your face. And then suddenly the train stops, a light comes on, and you look up." He snaps his fingers. "And there on the roof of the cave you see them—hundreds of drawings of mammoths, ibex, woolly rhinoceroses, and horses painted in red, tan, and black."

"Who painted them?"

I feel Léo shake his head. "No one knows."

"I want to see it."

Léo plays with a piece of my hair. "I'll take you."

I imagine myself doing things in France with Léo like characters in a romantic comedy. We carry balloons, eat croissants at a café, and kiss on bridges while French accordion music plays in the background.

His fingers brush against my cheek. "I would very much like to kiss you, Camille," he whispers. I can feel his breath on my face, his nose touching mine.

"I would very much like you to kiss me." I say this in a French accent, and then immediately regret it, hoping he doesn't think I'm making fun of him. But he smiles. And then he kisses me.

His mouth is soft, his kiss gentle. He doesn't press me back or shove his mouth on mine with all tongues and smashing lips like some boys do.

Léo stops kissing me, but he doesn't move back. He keeps his forehead against mine, his fingers light against my cheek. My heart melts into a puddle. "Kiss me again," I say. He does, and I never want it to stop. I want to stay on the bank forever, Léo holding me, hearing nothing but his breathing and the rush of the creek and the sound of the wind in the trees.

And then nausea hits me. My stomach starts to feel like a piece of paper being crumpled up into a ball, and I pull away from him.

"Camille?" Léo tries to take my hand, but I shake him loose. I sprint to the tree and throw up in the grass, puking my brains out to the point of tears. Léo is there at my side, patting my back.

"I'm okay," I say. "I'm sorry." I'm beyond embarrassed. I never puke, ever. Even when I'm sick.

"I think we should go to the . . . the clinic . . . what's the word? Hospital?"

"No, no, I'm okay," I say. I literally almost just threw up in this French boy's mouth. "I must have eaten something bad at the party. I have a really sensitive stomach."

Léo doesn't look convinced. "Still, I think I should take you, Camille."

"If it happens again, I promise I'll see a doctor." I'm trying my damnedest to sound casual.

He takes hold of my hands and rubs them between his own. "What can I do?"

"Gosh, I don't know? What's a guy to do after a girl pukes right after he kisses her?" I try to joke, but it falls flat and Léo doesn't laugh. "Um, you can walk me back?"

I try to act like it's no big deal. Like hey, this happens all the time, it's an American thing. But if it's possible to die of embarrassment, then I don't have much longer to live.

THREE

When we return to the party, Bea and Mateo are ready to leave. Léo and I sit in the back of Mateo's car, and Léo holds my hand the entire way. When Mateo pulls up to Léo's host parents' house, he gives me a quick hug. "I'll see you at Willow," he says. He gets out of the car and shuts the door, giving a little wave through the window. He stands on the drive with his hands in his pockets as we pull away. I watch until we turn the corner and I can't see him anymore.

Bea twists around in her seat. "Someone's got a boyfriend," she says in a singsong voice.

"Actually, I'm not so sure about that," I say. "I kind of threw up after he kissed me."

"What?" Mateo says. He starts laughing. "Only you, Camille."

"Yeah, thanks, Mateo," I say. "You're such a good friend."

"What happened?" Bea asks, alarmed. "Are you okay? Should I tell my mom? She'll know what to do."

"No, don't," I say. "I feel fine now. Your mom will make a big deal about it, and I'm embarrassed enough as it is."

"No kidding," Mateo says.

Bea punches him in the arm. "Stop it. Camille doesn't feel well. Have some compassion."

"So what happened?" Mateo asks. "I mean, after you puked on him."

"She didn't puke *on* him!" Bea says.

"I was too mortified to do anything but joke about it. I guess I'll see him at Willow? Maybe we'll go out or something. At least I hope that will happen."

"It will," Bea says. "Don't mention it. Pretend it never happened and it will all be okay."

I hope she's right, but I'd like to know how a girl could come back from puking in front of a guy she's crushing on.

It's late. When we get to Bea's house, we fall into bed right away, Bea on her twin bed under the window, and me on the matching bed that Bea has called mine since we first started having sleepovers in the fourth grade.

"So I noticed your parents didn't come," Bea says.

"Nope," I say, like I don't give a flying fuck. "Apparently, Mom had to take Chris to some science thing, and my dad fell asleep."

"Gosh, Camille, I'm sorry." Bea knows what my parents are

like, and it upsets her that they don't take me as seriously as they do Chris.

I shrug. "Whatever."

"Well, I'm excited that you get to spend a whole week with Léo at Willow!" Bea says.

"He's so cute, right? I wish you were going, too," I say.

"No way. I'll never be in the elite level," Bea says. "I'm not sure I ever want to be. It's, like, too much work, and I doubt I'll have the time, especially now that I'm a teen youth minister and all."

"Not everybody can do everything," I say.

"True dat," she says.

Silence.

"Um. Did you just say *true dat*?"

"Yeah," she says, and then bursts into laughter.

There's a knock on our door. "Girls, go to sleep," Bea's dad says.

"Good night, Camille," Bea whispers. Her bedsprings squeak as she turns over.

"Night, Bea," I whisper back.

Another stomachache wakes me up, and I have to run to the bathroom. I kneel in front of the toilet and hang my head over it, but I don't throw up this time. After a minute, the nausea stops and I go back to bed. I lie in a ball and hold my stomach. Bea's breathing and the little mumbles she makes when she sleeps seem louder than usual and I can't fall asleep. I don't know what this could be. Stomach flus don't last this long, and I don't think I ate anything to make me throw up this much. I reach under the pillow and take out my phone and tap *reasons for vomiting* into the search bar. A bunch of answers come up on Doctors.com: high blood pressure, food poisoning, flu, appendicitis, something called syncope . . . pregnancy.

My heart pounds, and my hands start to sweat. I start counting back on my phone's calendar. I missed my period in May, and I should have started a couple of days ago. I start turning cold. Really, really cold.

No. No, no, no, no, no.

I sit up. This can't be. No one gets pregnant on their first time. Or do they? I google it.

Yes, they do.

It only takes one eager sperm to hit an egg.

There's a movie they make everyone watch in health class that shows a cartoon of a bunch of sperm wiggling their way toward the cervix, through the uterus, and up the fallopian tubes, racing in a fertility marathon to be the first to get to that egg. Over and over in my head, I keep rolling that film. Is that what's going on in my body? If so, I'm at least *two months pregnant*.

I get up and tiptoe to Bea's bathroom. I pull my pajama shorts down and sit on the toilet. I hear Bea's dad cough, which makes me jump. The air conditioner clicks on, and cold air rushes out of the floor register and blows over my bare feet. I cross my arms and hug myself hard. The last time I felt this afraid of my body was when I started my period two years ago.

Maybe my period will start tomorrow, now that the stress of the play is over. I don't think I can stand to wait that long.

Hesitantly, I press my fists against my stomach, and then I push, increasing the pressure. I really don't know why I'm doing it, like I'm somehow going to "activate" my period by kneading my abs? Then, I push my forefinger in my vagina a little bit, to check if anything is coming out. My eye catches a framed photograph of Bea from fourth grade hanging just next to the door. Above it is a piece Bea cross-stitched back in seventh grade—it says HE IS RISEN. I am suddenly keenly aware that I am in my best friend's bathroom with my finger in my vagina. My best friend who never, ever, under any circumstances talks about her period. I take my finger out, but there isn't any blood.

Suddenly, there's a knock at the door. The yelp that escapes my mouth most certainly woke up the whole house.

"Camille, you okay in there?" Bea says through the door.

"Um, yeah! I'll be right out!" I flush the toilet and quickly wash my hands. I make a point of not looking at myself in the mirror.

When I open the door, Bea is standing there with a look of concern on her face. "Are you sure you're all right?"

"Oh, yeah. I thought I started my period, and I didn't want to get blood on your sheets." These are not words I ever say to Bea.

Bea's face pulls back in a grimace. "Camille, ew."

We crawl back into bed, and minutes later, I can tell Bea has fallen asleep.

I lie awake for the rest of the night.

FOUR
JUNE 30

An hour outside of our hometown, we see a billboard: WAF-FLE FACTORY AHEAD! Annabelle shakes her go-cup. "I need coffee. You mind if we stop at ye old Waffle Factory?"

"I could eat," I say. I look over my shoulder, and Bea is nodding.

Annabelle takes the exit to Waffle Factory; we park and go in. The restaurant echoes with the clatter of plates and conversation and smells like maple syrup and bacon. I find the bathroom, and when I come out, Annabelle's standing by the door, clutching a foam coffee cup. Bea is in the souvenir side of the store.

"It's like fifteen minutes for a table," Annabelle says. "I'm going to wait outside, okay?"

I nod and head into the souvenir store where Bea is looking

at a rack of jewelry charms, all hallmarks of Texas's pride: a tiny western boot, a Texas star, a cactus, a horse, a posy of bluebonnets.

"You would not believe the awesome junk in here, Camille," she says. She picks up a plastic western boot. The handle of a toilet brush pokes out of the top. "The spur even twirls." She spins the spur with the tip of her finger and grins.

Bea and I have always loved looking at kitschy knickknacks. We love going into dollar stores, thrift stores, and souvenir shops to look at the random stuff whose ridiculousness is undeniably adorable.

Today, at least for me, not so much. The fact that Bea can pretend nothing happened, that we'll go on being friends and doing goofy stuff we've always done, makes me angry. I look at that toilet brush. It's not cute. It's ugly and stupid and it's supposed to clean a toilet and that's all. I want to grab it out of her hands and hide it so no one can ever buy it to stick in some hunting cabin or whatever.

She pulls the brush out and waves it like a wand.

"That's the dumbest thing I ever saw," I say.

Her face falls. The spur wobbles to a stop.

"I know it's stupid, obvi," she says. "I was just trying to cheer you up."

"This sudden change of heart doesn't have anything to do with Annabelle helping me?"

She drops her arm, and the brush clatters to the floor.

"So that's a yes, then?"

She shakes her head, but she doesn't look at me.

"You weren't there for me, Bea. Do you know how excruciating it was to ask Annabelle Ponsonby, the person I admire more than anyone in the Globe community, including Mr. Knight, to help me? Do you know how that felt?"

She shrugs and flicks the spur again.

"There's no cheering me up, at least not for now," I say. "Laughing over a western boot with a toilet brush isn't going to make me forget that I'm pregnant and need to drive hours out of the way to get rid of it." I bend down, pick up the toilet brush, and shove it back into the boot.

FIVE
JUNE 24

I get dressed for acting class, put my hair into a ponytail. I pick up the Willow pin, which I'll have to give back to the Knights. I'll tell them that they made a mistake and that they should pick someone else to go to Willow. I'll have to text Léo and tell him I'm not coming and that we probably won't get a chance to see each other again, because he's leaving for France straight after Willow. He'll want to know why, and I won't have an answer. I'll never get a chance to take the little train into that cave with him. I'll never climb the stairs to the cathedral and look at the valley stretching out below, holding his hand, palm to palm in that old-fashioned way of his. Kids at the Globe will look at me like I'm the world's biggest idiot; that I gave up an opportunity they would kill to have. I'll be known as the girl who was too scared to go to Willow.

I pretend that it doesn't matter. That Willow isn't that great, that it's probably a drag having to do those embarrassing acting exercises like pretending to be a potato and making dumb faces. That the scouts and agents and college recruiters won't be interested in me. That the Knights make Willow sound cooler than it actually is. That Léo only wants a vacation girlfriend.

The Willow pin blurs in my vision, and then from nowhere I start crying hard. I put my hands over my mouth, but I can't stop the sobs from finding their way out. My face is wet with tears, my nose is running; the sadness and shame are washing out of me in water and snot.

I want so bad for someone to be here, to put their arms around me, to tell me I'm not alone, that I'm not a horrible person. The only person who has ever been able to do that for me is Bea.

I don't even realize that class has ended until Bea asks, "You need a ride home?"

"Actually, that'd be great. But can you give me a minute?"

"Sure!" she replies. "I'll be out front."

I watch her leave, dreading the conversation I have to have next. I go up to Mr. Knight and his wife, Tracy. "Hey, Tracy. Hi, Mr. Knight. Can I talk to you?"

"Camille! Just the young woman I was hoping to catch up with." Mr. Knight moves a stack of scripts over and sits on the corner of his desk. "Have you chosen your monologue for Leave?" Every actor going to Willow does a special monologue for an event called To Take a Tedious Leave, which is a quote from *The*

Merchant of Venice. I had planned on Helena's monologue from *A Midsummer Night's Dream*, but that's shot now.

"Actually, I've decided not to go to Willow." I take out the pin and set it on his desk.

Tracy looks at Mr. Knight and then at me. "This is a joke, right?" she says. "The camp is next week. Kiddo, you have to go. Willow is a huge honor and you deserve it."

Mr. Knight shakes his head. "Camille—"

"Please don't make me explain why," I say quickly. "I've made my mind up, and I'm not going."

"Nothing I can say will make you change your mind?" Mr. Knight says.

I stare at the ground and shake my head. Tracy takes the pin off the desk and then puts it back down. "I don't understand."

"I don't want to act anymore; I want to do other things. Do I always have to be the same?"

"No, you don't," Mr. Knight says. "But we wouldn't be doing our jobs if we didn't try to convince you to go. Are you coming back to the Globe?"

"I don't think there's any point," I whisper.

Mr. Knight reaches for the pin, turns it over in his fingers.

"I have to disagree," Tracy says. "Students with talent like yours are the reasons why we do this job. You are an excellent actor, Camille."

"I agree with Tracy," Mr. Knight says. "You're the best we have at the Globe right now. I think it bears saying that you have that extra something that other great actors have."

I wish they would take the pin and stop talking. "Thank you for the opportunity."

"I wish you the best, Camille." Mr. Knight holds out his hand.

I take his hand and we shake. Tracy doesn't say anything. She doesn't even look at me. I pick up my bag and head for the door.

I leave the theater, and I don't look back. All I want to do is go home, but I don't know what I'll do there. I spot Bea, and I really wish I hadn't accepted a ride.

She clomps over in the sky-high cork wedges she loves so much. Her dark ponytail swings back and forth, and the beaded purse that I bought for her birthday last month hangs over her shoulder. My best friend of more than ten years, and she has no idea what I'm going through.

"You ready?" She sits down and eases her feet out of her wedges. She examines a blister on her foot. "Why do the cutest shoes always cause the ugliest blisters?" Bea eases her shoe back on and then pulls out a bag of Oreos from her purse. Bea has carried a bag of Oreos with her since we were in elementary school. We always share those cookies, but now the chocolate smell wafting from the baggie makes me nauseous. "Want one?"

"No, thanks," I say. "Trying to lose some weight."

Bea takes one out and bites into it. "Are you okay? You never say no to an Oreo," she mumbles around the cookie.

It's because the idea of eating one makes me want to barf. Because I'm pregnant. I nearly say it. I *want* to say it. Bea is looking at me in that kind and trusting way, like she always does. And something inside me collapses.

"I need to tell you something," I blurt out before I can stop myself. "I had sex." Saying the word *sex* out loud startles me. It sounds so foreign and odd, as if I made the word up on the spot like Shakespeare always did. *Canker blossom, bodikins, flirt-gill.*

"Very funny." She bites into another cookie and starts crunching away.

"I'm not joking." I can feel my thighs starting to burn. I should have put sunscreen on. I don't know why I think this. Why should I care if my thighs get burned? I just told my best friend, who I know for a fact is a virgin and will be one until her wedding night, who is a teen youth minister at her church, who refuses to see an R-rated movie, who wears a silver purity ring, that I had sexual intercourse.

The crunching stops. "You had sex with Léo?" she whispers.

"No, not Léo. You don't know him."

"You had sex with someone I don't know?"

I don't respond, and she doesn't say anything. Her hand rests in her lap, an Oreo clutched in her fingers, half-eaten.

"I think the condom must have broken or something," I say finally.

"Condom," Bea says, trying out the word.

I made my best friend say *condom* out loud. I just did that.

"And I'm . . ." I swallow. "I'm pregnant, Bea. I don't know what to do. I—" Tears start to bubble up.

"Oh, Camille!" Bea drops the bag and the half-eaten cookie and throws her arms around me. I lean against her and cry, relieved that I've finally told someone, and that someone is my best friend. I clutch at her like she's a life raft and I've been drifting at sea for days.

"Don't worry, Camille. I won't let anything awful happen to

you, you know that." She reaches for her purse, pulls out a tissue. She dabs at the tears on my face. "So you're pregnant. You aren't the first girl to get pregnant on accident. You shouldn't have had sex, but you did. I promise you, I'll be there for you every step of the way, okay?"

The knot in my chest unties itself for the first time in days. I had nothing to be afraid of after all. I should have known she wouldn't judge me. I feel awful to have thought that. It will be okay. Bea will drive me to the clinic, hold my hand while I have the abortion, and then take me home after. She'll be there with Oreos and Cokes, and we'll watch dumb reality shows together. And then we'll go back to the way things were.

"I'll go to every appointment with you," she says. "I'll be your birthing coach, like you see on TV. I'll tell you to breathe and hold your hand and all that stuff. We'll figure it out together."

I haven't heard her right. "Bea . . . wait. I'm not having the baby."

Bea looks like I slapped her. "What do you mean, you're not having the baby?"

"I want to study theater like Annabelle. I don't want to be a mother at seventeen. I would sooner die. I have an appointment next week."

"To do what?"

"You know. Come on. Don't make me say it, Bea."

"I don't know what you're talking about."

"You know!"

Bea is shaking her head. "You can't. You can't kill your baby."

"Stop saying *baby*! It's not a baby, and it never will be. I gave

up Willow for this. I'll never know Léo. So that tells you everything, okay?"

Bea won't stop shaking her head.

Mateo pulls up in the parking lot, rolls the window down,
and calls out to us. "Hey, ladies. Your chariot awaits."

Bea whispers, "I don't . . . I . . . Do your parents know?"

"No. And I'm not going to tell them. I don't want anyone to
know. Please don't tell." I reach out, but she shrugs me away and
stands up.

"I won't. I won't tell." She goes over to Mateo and stops in
front of his car. Her arms are crossed and her shoulders are
hunched forward. She's crying.

I'm frozen solid, stuck to the bench like it's a theater seat and
I'm in the audience waiting for the next scene to unfold.

The door opens, and Mateo steps out of the car. He ducks
down to make eye contact with her and brushes her tears away
with his thumbs like an actor in a Nicholas Sparks movie. She says
something, and he looks my way. I can't see his expression, but he
doesn't wave me over. He talks to Bea. He hugs her. She shakes
her head. He puts his arm around her, comforting her, and helps
her in the car.

I stand up. I start toward the car, and then I stop. No one is
looking at me. I wait, like a dog that's been left behind, unable to
understand that she's been abandoned. I sit down again and watch
the car, hoping Bea will get out and come back. I picture her
running toward me with her arms outstretched, wanting to help,
wanting to comfort me.

But she doesn't, and the car pulls away.

SIX

JUNE 30

I leave the souvenir shop and go out into the lobby of the restaurant and sit on a bench with other waiting diners.

A few minutes later, Bea comes out of the shop. She leans against the wall by the bench.

Annabelle comes in and tosses her cup into the trash. She gives us each a look. "Uh, what did I miss?"

"Nothing," Bea and I say at the same time.

Finally, the hostess calls our name. We follow her to a booth, and she drops three menus on the table.

Annabelle picks up a coffee mug. "Oh my god, hurry up, people. I need fuel here, stat." She waves the cup in the air, looking around the room for a waitress.

"You just had coffee, like, two seconds ago," Bea says. "You must like it a lot."

Annabelle sighs and looks lovingly at her coffee cup. "So much."

"Did you drink tea in England?"

"I tried to, but it didn't take. I went straight back to my first love." Annabelle points at a woman all alone, dressed in denim shorteralls and a plaid shirt. She looks like she could out-bench-press most of the guys in the restaurant. "See her over there? What do you think her story is?"

Bea looks. "Oh, that's Marge. She drives a truck."

Annabelle nods. "Like a boss." She gestures with her head. "That dude at the counter with the clip-on tie and short sleeves."

"You mean Fred?"

"Fred's your man if you're looking to buy . . . ," I say.

"Baby dolls," Annabelle says, perfectly deadpan.

Bea and I look at each other and burst out laughing. She reaches out to take my hand, but I pull it away.

A waitress comes by and fills Annabelle's coffee cup. She looks at my mug, still upside down on its frilled paper doily.

"Can I have a Sprite, please?" I ask.

"Sure, honey," she says. "Girls, our special today is waffles with bacon and a side of home fries."

"I'll have that," I say.

"Same," Annabelle says.

"Make it three," Bea says.

The waitress picks up our menus, taps them square on the table. She winks at us and goes off.

Bea sighs happily and sits back in her seat. "I love her."

"The only person I let call me honey are Waffle Factory wait-resses," Annabelle says. "Especially if they are named Flo."

"Or Alice," I chime in. "Alice can even call me sweetie."

"Betty can call me toots, but only if I'm ordering pie," Annabelle says.

"And only if she has a pencil behind her ear and those really comfortable white shoes," Bea says.

Annabelle smiles. "Gotta love those sensible white shoes."

I realize that I have no idea what story Bea told her parents to be able to come on this road trip. "Bea, where do your mom and dad think you are?"

"I told them I was going to look at some colleges with the two of you. So if we could maybe, like, drive by a college, I'll feel better about lying to them."

My best friend never lies, especially to her parents. But she did so to be with me. I'm not sure what to do with that.

"What about you?" Bea asks me.

"Oh, uh, they think I'm at Willow."

A quiet falls over the table.

A van pulls into a parking space by the window, and two adults and six kids get out.

Annabelle nods toward the family. "See that family?"

"The Funkweiler family?" Bea asks.

"Those guys are hard-core Christians."

"Nah, they are in one of those German accordion bands—" Bea says.

"No, I mean, seriously. They are as Christian as you can get. You can tell from the way they're dressed—those awful calf-length denim skirts and sneakers. The girls always have French braids and the boys always have crew cuts." She dumps two cups of creamers into her coffee and three packs of sugar. "It's their jam."

Bea's smile fades. She falls quiet.

"The lady at the crisis center dressed like that," I say.

Bea shoots a look at me. "What's a crisis center? When did you go to a crisis center?"

I don't answer her.

"Crisis centers are Christian organizations that trick women into thinking the clinic is a real clinic, but in reality they are sham clinics that pressure women out of having abortions and treat them like shit to boot," Annabelle says. "They lecture them on the Bible and spout all kinds of bullshit about pregnancy and birth control. It's a trap, it's meant to be a trap, and Camille fell into it."

SEVEN
JUNE 23

There are no other patients in the waiting room when I come in. It doesn't look like a medical office at all, which takes away some of my nerves. It's painted a soft pink and carpeted with a green rug, and a group of tall houseplants in yellow ceramic pots sits in one corner. A woman with a pixie haircut is behind the check-in counter. She looks like a lady from Bea's church, Ruth . . . something.

Please don't let it be Ruth.

She looks up from her computer and smiles when she sees me.

"You must be Camille," she says. "I'm Jean. We spoke on the phone. How are you doing, darlin'? Feeling any better?"

I breathe a sigh of relief. "I'm okay."

"I was so worried about you," Jean says. "My Bible study group has been praying for you."

What she says doesn't bother me because so many people in Texas are religious. But it seems strange to me that someone like her would want to work in a family planning clinic.

"How come there aren't any protestors here?" I say. "I was worried about that."

"Oh, they don't bother us," Jean says. She hands over a clipboard and asks me to fill in the information. I sit in one of the chairs. It asks the usual medical information, but I hesitate over the personal stuff like my address and emergency contact number.

"Excuse me, Jean? How confidential is this form?"

"No one will know but us, hon."

At the end of the form is a question: *What do you expect from this visit?* I write in: *I would like to schedule an abortion.*

I hand it to Jean and sit down. I take my cell phone out to check my messages and Jean pipes up: "Darlin', it's clinic policy to turn your cell phone off. It interferes with our equipment."

"Oh, I'm sorry." I switch off my phone. A little TV across from me comes on and a video starts. A fetus floating in a uterus flashes on the screen. "Life is a miracle," a man narrates.

I stand up and pretend to be interested in the plants. They're fake.

A woman comes from the back dressed in pink scrubs. She's holding my folder. "Hi, Camille," she says. "I'm Lisa. You want to come with me?"

I follow Lisa in her pink scrubs down the hallway.

"How's the weather out there?"

"Um, it's hot," I say.

She pauses by a scale and I set my purse down, take off my shoes, and stand on it. I'm ten pounds heavier than the last time I weighed myself. I flush with embarrassment, but Lisa doesn't say anything. She makes a note in my file and leads me down a short hallway and into a darkened room. "Undress from the waist down and then sit on the table." She hands me a sheet. "Cover up with this. I'll be right back."

I take off my shorts and underwear. I hesitate over my socks. I don't think it would matter if I left them on, but she said everything from the waist down, so I take my socks off, too.

The tile floor is freezing, and my feet are cold by the time I sit down. The paper on the table rustles underneath me. I spread the sheet over my knees and tuck it around my waist.

Lisa comes back into the room and sits on a rolling stool. She takes out a long plastic rod and rolls what looks like a condom on it. "You can lie down now. This won't take but a minute."

"I . . . What is that?" I say.

"It's an ultrasound probe, hon. It's the best way to confirm the age of your baby," she says. "It has to go in your vagina, okay?"

My heart starts to pound. "Do we have to do this?"

She doesn't hear me. "Put your feet in the stirrups there and lie back."

I do as she says. I lie back and set my feet carefully in the little metal hooks at the bottom of the table. They've covered them with baby socks—one pink, one blue.

Stirrups used to mean horses and trail rides and friends. Now stirrups mean ultrasounds and god-awful-looking probes.

"I'm gonna hand it to you, and you put it in. Just like putting in a tampon, okay?"

I take it, embarrassed beyond words. I slide it in. It's cold and gooey.

She takes the handle from me and moves the probe back and forth; I can feel it swiping around. I stare up at the ceiling. There's a sign up there that says JESUS LOVES YOU. The ultrasound machine is making this loud humming noise, and when Lisa moves, her stool squeaks. There's a pineapple-shaped wax melter on the table next to me, and the fake tropical fumes wafting out of it are the kind that give me an instant headache. I turn my head away from it and try to hold my breath.

Lisa swipes the probe around some more. She's taking forever, and I hope this means she doesn't see anything. I hope the pregnancy test is wrong. Maybe it will be okay. I cross my fingers and then uncross them. *Stupid.*

"I love this job," Lisa says. "It's like opening a present at Christmas, seeing the baby for the first time. It's such a miracle."

I wish she wouldn't call it a baby.

She taps something onto the keyboard on the machine. "There!" she says. "There's your baby."

My heart sinks. It's true, and there's no running away from it now.

She turns the screen toward me. "Here she is. Or he. We can't tell the sex just yet. You'll know that in a few weeks. Unless you want it to be a surprise when you deliver. Are you hoping for a girl or a boy?"

I stare up at the ceiling. I won't look. I don't want to see it.

"Look at that teeny little miniature baby."

I shrug.

"You don't want to see your baby?" she says in disbelief.

I shake my head.

"You have to look," Lisa says with warning. "It's Texas law. If you don't look, then you have to pay for the exam, and it's four hundred dollars."

I look. The picture on the screen is black and white. In the middle is a round blank space with a white shape, which Lisa points to. She smiles.

"This is your baby here. You can see she has little arms and legs, and her heart fluttering, that means it's beating. Isn't that exciting?"

I stare at the ceiling again. "Not really," I say.

"A heartbeat, it's a love beat, we say in the clinic. Just like that cheesy old seventies song."

"When can I schedule it?"

"Schedule what, hon?" she replies.

"The procedure." My voice doesn't sound like mine at all. I don't know whose it is.

Lisa says nothing.

"And I've never heard of that song," I whisper.

Lisa prints out a copy of the ultrasound and puts it in my folder, but her friendliness is gone. I pull out the probe and hand it to her. She does whatever she has to do with it to make it ready for the next person, hands me a washcloth, and leaves.

I sit up and wipe myself off.

I get dressed. There's a butt-shaped wrinkle in the paper on the table where I was sitting. I tear it off, bunch it into a ball, and cram it into the trash can.

No one comes back in, so I pick up my purse and go out in the hall. I stand there. After a few minutes, Lisa appears and gestures for me to follow her into an office. She leaves the folder on the desk, steps back into the hall, and closes the door behind her without saying a word to me.

I hear whispers in the hallway. I make out Lisa saying something about me being determined to have an abortion. There's a rustling of paper and then footsteps walking away.

I didn't do a good enough job cleaning the ultrasound goo off, and I can feel my underwear sticking to it. I cross my arms over my chest. It's cold in the office. What's taking so long? I'm the only one in the clinic. I'm going to be late for work, and Iggy will yell at me.

A silver digital picture frame sits on the corner of the desk. I watch as a photo of a couple and two elementary-school-age boys dissolves into a photo of the family standing in front of Sleeping Beauty's Disneyland castle.

I reach for my phone for something to do, but I remember I'm not supposed to turn it on. There is a stack of pink and blue pamphlets on a table next to me, so I pick one up. The information inside is about all the side effects of an abortion, things like breast cancer, suicide, and hysterectomy from a punctured uterus. I put the pamphlet down.

Finally, a woman comes in—it's the lady from the pictures. The rims of her flesh-colored peds are visible inside her black patent leather flats. Her chin-length soccer mom bob is hair-sprayed perfectly in place.

"Hello, Camille." She sits down at the desk. "I'm Susan Clark, your pregnancy counselor."

"Hi."

"So we know you're pregnant, that's definitely positive from the ultrasound." She speaks carefully, trying to meet my eyes, but I won't look at her.

"Do you want to tell me how this happened? Sometimes it's very comforting to tell someone."

"I . . ." I glance at Susan. "Do I have to?"

"It's important," she says. "It gives us a picture of who you are and how we can help you. What you tell me stays here in my office. This is a safe place."

I clear my throat. "Um . . . well, I was dating this guy, and we hooked up. We used a condom, but I don't know what happened to it."

"Unfortunately, condoms don't work very well. Condoms fail at least fifty percent of the time, so I'm not surprised it broke." She pulls my folder toward her. "Most birth control does fail, including birth control pills. The only one hundred percent way of being sure you'll never get pregnant is to wait to have sex until you're ready to have a baby, right?" She nods, her eyebrows raised, as though I've done something really wrong. "You know the mistake you made, right?" Again, the raised eyebrows and the nod.

"I don't think that's right about condoms," I say quietly. I try to think back to tenth grade when we had sex ed, but no one talked about contraception.

She stares at me.

I feel stupid, but more than that, I feel shamed.

"Now you know. And now you can do better going forward from here, right?" Susan finishes all her questions with the word *right*. Like I agree with her completely.

Susan opens my folder and goes through the information. She's taking forever. I shift in my chair.

"I have to get to work," I say. But it's like she doesn't hear me.

She flips the pages to the ultrasound picture. She smiles and turns it so I can see. "Look at that little miracle—" she says.

"I think there's a mistake," I say, interrupting her.

She looks at the name on my folder. "You're Camille Winchester, right?"

"That's my name, yes."

"Looks like your due date will be—"

"I don't need to know the due date because I'm not having it."

"It?" Susan says. "What is *it*?"

I swallow. "The . . ."

"Baby?" Susan says. "Because it is a baby, you know that, Camille, right?"

"I guess I should have said on the phone. I think Jean misunderstood." I bunch my hands in my lap. This is bad. I should have spoken up and told them right away instead of assuming they knew I wanted an abortion. Now I'll probably have to pay for that ultrasound, and I only have a few dollars in my purse.

"Well, let's chat about that," she says. Her voice is calm and she forms each word perfectly. "God sent you here to us, and we want to look after you. Now, you have other options for your little one, and I'd like you to know what they are before you jump to a decision you may regret later in your life, right?" She comes around to my side of the desk and sits on the chair opposite me. She leans forward and puts her hands over mine. "We can help you find a wonderful deserving Christian family to adopt your baby, or you can keep her and raise her yourself. Both of these decisions will give her the same chance at life that your mother gave you. Can I tell you a little bit more about how we can help?"

Four hundred dollars, I think. I'll owe that if I don't listen. So I nod.

"It looks like you're three months pregnant." She reaches into a wicker basket on the table and takes out a little doll. "This is what your baby looks like now." The tiny figure has a face and little arms and legs.

"I'm not that far along," I say.

She sets the figure on my lap. "It's very hard to tell the exact age."

"But that can't be—"

"Now, the first step is to keep you safe, happy, and healthy. Our school for expectant mothers will protect you from people who might try to make you feel bad for your decision. We also have a dormitory if you feel unsafe or unwelcome in your home. In addition, we'll teach you important mommy skills like baby care and budgeting. We also offer vocational skills at the school like retail sales, waitressing, housekeeping, to help you earn money."

Over on the picture frame, a photo of a lady's birthday party slides into view. Her grayish blond hair is tightly curled, and she looks like an older version of Susan Clark.

"I'm not dropping out of my school," I say. "Why would I do that?"

Susan stands and reaches up to take a pamphlet off the shelf. "We find it's for the best. Our girls made the terrible decision to give themselves to boys before marriage, and they have to deal with that. Bullying only adds fuel to the fire. Our school is the best option."

"I don't want to drop out of my high school," I say again, this time more firmly. "I want to finish my senior year and go to college. I don't want to have a baby."

"I know you feel that way now," she says. "But once you hold your baby in your arms and see her little face for the first time, you'll realize you've done the right thing. Don't you want to do the right thing, Camille?"

"I . . . of course, but—"

"What if your mother had aborted you? Have you ever thought of that?"

"My mother resents me," I blurt out. "She had to give up her dream of being a pastry chef when she had me. If my mom had aborted me, she'd be living her dream. So . . ."

Susan's face hardens.

"Why is my life more important than hers?" I whisper.

She slides the pamphlet across the desk. "To take a life, a little innocent baby's life, is tantamount to murder. I think you need to think a little harder about this decision. It's proven that abortion can cause terrible mental health issues for you like depression and suicide, and physical problems down the road like uterine perforations and infertility. It can also cause painful periods for the rest of your life."

I shouldn't have yelled at her like that. Now she'll kick me out and force me to pay. "Can I just schedule the . . . procedure? Please?"

"You can't say the word out loud?" She looks me right in the eye, her face expressionless. "Abortion."

I meet her gaze, but I don't reply.

"We are here for mothers, not murderers. I think the next step for us is to contact your parents." She reaches for the phone. She opens my folder. I see my mom's cell phone number under emergency contact.

I stand up and snatch my folder from under Susan's hand; the doll tumbles to the floor. I race out of the room.

"That folder is clinic property," Susan shouts.

I cram the folder into my backpack on top of my Iggy's uniform and push the door open.

I'm halfway down the street when I hear footsteps behind me. I'm scared it's Susan or Lisa running after me to make me pay for the ultrasound and to get my folder back. But it's Jean. She's holding a bag with tissue poking out of the top.

"I want you to have this," Jean says. "It's a little something I made for you the night you called." She hands the bag to me. "You get in touch if you need anything, Camille. I mean that."

When I get to work, I look inside the bag. Under the tissue paper is a pair of pink-and-blue knitted baby booties with little tassels. I find a trash can and shove the booties underneath a pile of wrappers smeared with ketchup and chili cheese.

EIGHT

JUNE 30

"See?" Annabelle says to Bea. "I told you it was a trap. And there are tons of those fake clinics around. Way more than there are real family planning clinics."

"But that can't be true." Bea looks at me, bewildered. "How can that be right?"

I don't say anything. I can't even begin to answer her.

The family from the van is seated at a table next to us. The mom smiles at me.

The waitress comes over and sets plates in front of us. Annabelle scrapes the whipped cream off her waffles and flicks it to the side of her plate. She drowns the waffles in butter and syrup and then slides the pitcher across to us. Bea syrups her waffles and passes the pitcher to me.

I can't stop looking at that family.

When their waffles arrive, they hold hands and bow their heads over their waffles. The father starts saying grace. He has a booming voice, and he's saying the prayer so loud, everyone in the restaurant can hear.

"Dear Lord, we thank you for this bounty you've placed before us, and we ask you to give us strength to pray for the sinners in the world who have turned their faces from you. In your name we pray."

The father finishes his prayer, and the family begins to eat their waffles.

The waitress comes back to refill Annabelle's coffee cup and notices my plate. "Anything wrong with your waffles, sweetheart?"

"My stomach hurts a little," I say.

"I'll get you another Sprite—that always settles the tummy. And I'll box these up for you in case you get hungry later." She picks up my plate and goes off.

I glance at the church family again.

The parents are looking at us and whispering to each other. The man leans in, his hand over his mouth like a little kid telling a secret. His wife nods, her lips pressed into a line. She's looking at Annabelle's Wendy Davis T-shirt.

"It's your T-shirt," I say.

Annabelle looks down at her shirt, confused. "What about it?" She pulls at it. "Do I have syrup on it?"

"Those people are looking at your T-shirt." I half stand up, then sit down.

Annabelle leans back in the booth. "I hope my T-shirt sears their retinas. I hope they can't unsee it."

The mother reaches into her purse and hands a paper to the littlest girl, who is maybe six years old or so, and points at Annabelle. The girl comes over to our table. She holds out a little pamphlet.

I take it, even though she was trying to give it to Annabelle— it's a little comic book about hell. In the first cell, the devil is forking people into a fire with a pitchfork. The caption underneath it reads: "Fornicators and abortionists are damned to hell."

"Jesus loves you," the little girl says before skipping back to her seat.

Bea sits stock-still.

"What did she give you?" Annabelle says. She leans forward and pulls the comic out of my hand. "What the fuck," she whispers.

"She just loves spreading the word," the mother says to us.

Annabelle slides out of the booth and stands up. "Let's go, okay?"

I fumble in my purse for money.

"Don't worry. I got this." Annabelle drops money onto the table.

"I'm not like that," I hear Bea say to herself as we leave the restaurant. "I know I'm not like that."

We're flying down the highway. Annabelle is in her groove, alternatively changing the radio dial and switching lanes. That cheesy Carrie Underwood song, "Jesus, Take the Wheel," comes on.

"What about keeping your hands on the wheel instead?" Annabelle says. "Turn into the skid, idiot."

I'm happy we are on our way, but my bladder has other ideas. "Can you please pull over? I am about to pee myself."

Annabelle rolls her eyes but takes the nearest exit. "You just peed at Waffle Factory, but fine. I'll fill up the car."

I jump out of the car as soon as it comes to a stop and run into the shop. When I come out of the bathroom, I pass two guys by the refrigerated section pulling out tallboys of Red Bull. They're maybe twenty or so. Both wear battered cowboy hats and old faded western shirts.

I look through the aisles for some Mike and Ikes and cheese crackers. I find them and get in line behind the guys in cowboy hats. The door dings and Annabelle comes in, holding her go-cup. "I'm going to get some coffee," she says to me.

"Hey," one of the guys says to her. "Get me some coffee, too."

She ignores him and goes over to the bank of coffee machines.

"Smile much?" the guy yells.

"Whoa, she is hot," his friend says.

"Face is okay," he replies. "But her ass is something else."

My shoulders tense up, and I look down at the floor.

The boys pay and leave with their tallboys. I step forward to pay for my junk food. The woman behind the counter shakes her head. "Jerks," she mutters under her breath.

Annabelle returns with a large cup of coffee in her hand, her eyes on her phone. Bea trails behind her, holding a box of Dunkaroos.

"Are you buying more food?" Annabelle asks her. "You brought an entire pantry with you practically."

"But they have Dunkaroos." She points at the box. "You can't find these things *anywhere*."

"Let's stay in here until those guys leave," I say.

"What guys?" Annabelle says, cramming her phone in her back pocket.

"The guys who were in line ahead of me," I say. "They were talking about you."

Annabelle glances out the window. The guys are standing outside by the ice freezer drinking their Red Bulls. "I don't care about those dudes. Let's go."

We go outside, and the guys immediately notice. The one in the blue shirt is squatting with his back against the wall. The other is leaning against the freezer.

"Sorry my friend yelled at you," Blue Shirt says. "He has Tourette's syndrome when he sees a hot girl."

"That's not funny," Annabelle says. "My sister has Tourette's."

Blue Shirt pushes himself away from the wall. "Aw, hey, I'm sorry. I didn't mean anything. Just a joke."

"Whatever," she says.

Blue Shirt shades his eyes against the sun and looks Annabelle up and down. "Really? Your sister has Tourette's?"

"No, but that doesn't mean you get to make fun of other people's afflictions."

"You got me there," he says. "I'm Billy, and this ugly-looking dude up against the freezer is Justin. You girls up for hanging out?"

"We have to get going," I say. "We're supposed to be some-where by dark."

"It's not even noon yet," Justin says. "You can get to your somewhere in plenty of time." He pulls a joint out of his pocket and waves it at us. He raises his eyebrows.

I shake my head. "Really, it's nice of you . . ."

"Can I have one of them Dunkaroos?" he says to Bea, pointing at the box with his joint. "I haven't seen those in years."

She steps back, clutching her box so hard she's denting it.

"What's the matter? Don't you talk?"

Bea turns away.

"Uptight much?" Billy says.

"Leave her alone," I say.

Justin holds the joint out to Annabelle.

"No, thanks," Annabelle says.

"Come on," Justin says. "Don't be that way."

"I am that way."

"What, you never smoked a joint before?"

"I don't have to explain why," Annabelle says. "The 'no, thanks' should be sufficient."

"Jesus Christ, don't be so uptight," Billy says. "Justin's trying to be nice, sharing his weed with you and all, and you're acting all shitty."

"Let me give you some advice," Annabelle says. "When a girl says she doesn't want to do something, guess what? She doesn't want to do it."

"I'm sorry," I say to them.

"Don't apologize to them," Annabelle says to me, but I ignore her.

"We're in a hurry," I add. "Come on, Bea."

"Yeah, go on, *Bea*," Billy says. He's not smiling. I don't like the look in his eyes, like a snake about to strike. He reaches into his shirt pocket and takes out a cigarette and lights it.

We head to the car. "Damn, Annabelle," I whisper. "Why did you have to say that?"

"Why did you apologize? I hate dudes like that."

"I hate guys like that, too, but I'd rather just avoid them."

Bea chucks her box of Dunkaroos in a nearby trash can.

"See you later, bitches," one of the boys calls out.

"Assholes," Bea throws over her shoulder. I look at her, mouth open. I have never in my life heard Bea swear.

"Hey, she talks," Justin says. "The little mouse can speak!" He starts to laugh.

But Billy doesn't share in the joke. He stands up, flicking the cigarette away from him. "What did you say?"

Bea turns around and walks backward. "What are you, deaf? I said you and your friend are *assholes*." And then she flips them the bird. Both hands.

And then we run.

Bea piles into the back seat and slides across it as Annabelle whips out of the gas station.

"Wow, that felt *great*!" Bea says. She sits up and puts her seat belt on.

"Oh my god!" Annabelle bursts out laughing. "That was hilarious. I was living for the look on their faces when you flipped them off. Priceless."

"I bet they thought you were the harmless one, Bea," I say.

"I didn't expect any of that to happen," she says, breathless.

"Normally I walk past guys like that, but sometimes you gotta recognize a teachable moment," Annabelle says.

"Think they will fix their behavior?" I ask Annabelle.

She rolls her eyes. "No, but it makes me feel better."

Annabelle flips through her phone and puts on Beyoncé's "Run the World."

"Anthem time, ladies."

We start singing along at the top of our lungs, and even Bea joins in. She doesn't know the words so she starts making up her own: "Freaks and freaks and boys are jerks and why did I throw my Dunkaroos away!"

Beyoncé gets to the part about Houston, Texas, and we whoop and sing as loud as we can.

Annabelle looks in her rearview mirror. She turns off the radio. Bea is still singing. "Hey," Bea says.

"Oh shit," Annabelle says.

"What?" I say.

"Those guys," she says. "I think they're following us."

Bea and I look out the back window. A bright red Jeep is speeding down the lane behind us.

"Are you sure that's them?" Bea asks.

Annabelle switches lanes and the Jeep follows, flashing its headlights. Annabelle moves into the far-right lane. "I'm willing to bet yes, that is them."

"Oh my god," I say, turning back around. "What the hell? What should we do?"

The Jeep moves into the lane next to ours and pulls right alongside our car.

"Don't look at them," I say. "Scrunch down in your seat, Bea."

"I shouldn't have done that. I shouldn't have called them assholes. This is what I get for swearing!"

I see Billy lower his window and stick his hand out the window, middle finger raised.

"Good lord, these guys must have tiny dicks." Annabelle slows down, and they slow down, too.

Traffic zooms around us. No one pays attention. No one looks.

"Why are they doing this?" Bea cries.

"Because they *are* assholes," Annabelle says, her voice tense. "Just like you said."

Annabelle speeds up. They speed up.

Annabelle is gripping the steering wheel hard. Her mouth is tight.

I take out my phone. "Should I call the cops?"

"I don't know," Annabelle says.

I punch in the numbers 9-1-1, my thumb hovering over the screen, about to place the call.

The Jeep pulls ahead of us and swerves into our lane. Annabelle sucks in her breath and jerks the steering wheel. We skid onto the verge, gravel flying. I start screaming. Bea is screaming. There's a popping noise, and the car jerks to a stop.

Annabelle's face is white, and her eyes are as wide as dinner plates.

"Jesus, take the wheel!" I blurt out.

Annabelle stares at me for a second, and then I burst

into laughter. Annabelle sits back in her seat, laughing and crying at the same time, wiping tears away with the back of her hand.

Bea pats Annabelle on the shoulder. "That was some good driving," she says.

"Poor Buzzi," I say. "I hope she's all right."

Bea turns in her seat. "Someone's coming."

A big white pickup truck with shiny chrome pulls up behind us. A man and woman get out and run to our car.

I roll down my window. "You girls okay?" he asks.

The woman leans over him. "We saw the whole thing," she says. "That Jeep drove you right off the road. Do y'all want us to call the cops?"

"It's fine, we're okay," Bea says. "Those boys are long gone anyway."

"Your tire ain't okay," the man says. "Looks like you had a blowout when you came off the highway."

The three of us get out of the car. He's right; the front passenger-side tire is a shredded pancake.

The man squats down and examines the tire. "I can change it for you. You gotta spare?"

Annabelle nods.

"There's a tire store a little bit up yonder where you can get a replacement," he tells us.

"Can't we drive on the spare?" I ask. We've already lost so much time.

"Nah, it's not good to drive on those doughnut tires." He picks at the rubber. "Looks like y'all had some dry rot. Probably caused that blowout. You should probably get a whole new set of tires."

"A new set?" Annabelle's voice catches.

"How much do you think a new tire will cost, Hank?" the woman says, glancing at Annabelle.

He thinks for a moment. "Oh, about a hundred bucks for the one tire."

"I can pay for it, Annabelle," Bea says. "I can call my mom. I mean, it's my fault those boys ran us off the road."

"You girls go sit in the truck with Tammy," Hank says, his voice gentle. "It's safer there away from traffic. Tammy, get them girls a Coke."

"Can I stay?" Annabelle asks. "I want to watch you change the tire, if you don't mind. I'd like to learn."

Hank pushes his hat back on his head. "Why, sure. I don't mind a bit."

Hank starts to change our tire while Tammy takes us to the truck. SWEETWATER QUARTER HORSES is lettered on the sides.

I pull Bea aside. "You can't call your mom, you know that, right?"

Bea looks confused. "Why? She'll pay for the tire with her credit card over the phone."

"I don't want your mom or my mom involved in any of this because they might tell us to turn around and come home. And anyway, you've got to quit expecting your mom to wave a magic money wand and fix everything every time you have a problem." I say this kind of hard, and then I immediately regret it. It's not Bea's fault she's so sheltered, and that her parents do everything for her.

Her shoulders slump. "I'm sorry, Camille. I didn't think."

"No worries, okay? I can cover the cost of the tire. I think my paycheck will be deposited today anyway."

We get in the back of the truck. Tammy is sitting in the passenger seat.

"I'm sure sorry that happened to you girls," Tammy says. She rummages around in a cooler on the floor and hands us each a Coke. "Those boys were hell-bent on running you off the road. Y'all know them from high school or something?"

"No. We saw them at the gas station earlier," Bea says. "They were kind of harassing us."

I crack open the can and take a drink. The cold feels good on my throat. Bea doesn't open her Coke. She holds it in her hands and stares out the window at the traffic swooping by.

Tammy hooks her elbow over the seat. "Boys like that remind me of my ex-husband. You girls going far?"

"Kind of," I say. "We're going to a flea market in the Rio Grande Valley."

Her face brightens. "Hidalgo flea market?"

"You know it?"

"I sure do. Lots of good stuff there. Alamo is a sweet little town. Have you been to the wildlife refuge?"

Tammy proceeds to tell us about all the birds and butterflies that pass through. I know she's trying to take our minds off what happened, but Bea isn't saying a word. She looks defeated, like someone pulled the plug on her and all her energy drained out.

"What's the matter, honey?" Tammy asks.

"I shouldn't have said anything to those boys," Bea says. "It's all my fault we got run off the road."

"It's okay, Bea," I say. I put my arm around her shoulders. "It's only a tire. Nobody died."

"But that's the point," Bea says. "We *could* have died. We don't know what those boys meant to do."

"Sugar, being run off the road ain't your fault at all," Tammy says. "Don't you think that, okay? No matter what you said to those boys, you didn't deserve to be treated like that."

"You don't know what I said," Bea insists. "I called them assholes and then I put up my middle finger. Both hands!"

"Now you listen to me, Bea," Tammy says. "If those boys could see you now, they'd be happy as clams. They want you to cry; they want you upset. Are you going to let them win?"

"I guess you're right."

"You kick the dust off your feet now and forget about those boys."

Tammy starts talking about her horses, and I tell her about the horse camp Bea and I used to go to.

"My Jesus money!" Bea blurts out. "I can pay for the tire."

Tammy looks startled. "Jesus money?"

"Bea keeps a hundred dollars behind a picture of Jesus in her wallet at all times," I explain to Tammy. "She's supposed to use it if she meets someone in need."

"I just love that," Tammy says. "A hundred dollars behind Jesus. Bea, you are as sweet as all get out."

Finally, Bea smiles.

Hank returns to the truck, sweat pouring down his face.

Annabelle stands behind him; her hands are filthy and there's a smudge of dirt on her cheek, but she looks triumphant. Tammy hands them both wet wipes from the glove compartment, followed by cans of Cokes. Tammy and Hank are prepared for everything.

"You're good to go, girls," Hank says. "Now you take the next exit and make a right at the light. You'll see the tire store on the next corner. Tell Dale that Hank sent you. He'll give you a good price."

"How long do you think it will take to fix?" I ask.

"Oh, say an hour? Dale's real fast."

We get out of the truck, and Hank and Tammy walk us back to our car.

"Thank you," Annabelle says. "I don't know what we would have done without your help."

"Happy to be of service." Hank puts his arm around Tammy.

Tammy and Hank say goodbye and return to their truck. Hank holds the door open for Tammy. He makes sure she's safe inside with her seat belt on before he shuts the door.

I watch them pick up speed on the verge and move onto the highway. I'm sorry to see them go.

NINE

Inside the tire store, a guy around my dad's age dressed in brown Carhartt pants and a shirt with FAST TIRE embroidered on the pocket is standing behind the counter. A toothpick dangles from the corner of his mouth.

Annabelle goes up to the counter. "We're looking for Dale?"

"You found him," the man says. "Help you girls?"

"Um, yeah," I say. "A guy called Hank told us to come. We need a tire."

"Model, make, and year?"

"It's a 2007 Ford Focus," Annabelle says.

Dale types one-fingered onto a keyboard smeared with grease and frowns at the computer. He leans against the counter and rubs his chin. "We're outta tires here for that make, but I probably have it at the warehouse." He taps the keyboard and squints at it. "Looks like they can get that tire on the truck . . . that should take you . . ." He chews on the toothpick for a second. "Be outta here about four—no later'n six. That sound all right?"

"I thought this place was called Fast Tire," Annabelle says.

"I'm sorry, girls. Best I can do for you. You can go on and wait in the customer lounge. There's free coffee and a TV. Coupla doughnuts might be left."

Dale charges us ninety dollars for the tire, which includes Hank's discount. Bea hands over her Jesus money.

They take our car into the garage. The flat tire flaps.

"Poor Buzzi," Annabelle says. "She didn't deserve that."

We trudge across the street to a little kids' playground. Annabelle leans against a slide and Bea sits on a swing.

"Why do guys have to be like that?" I ask.

Annabelle snorts. "That's the question of the universe."

"I can't imagine girls running people off the road," I say.

"Because they wouldn't."

"Hank was nice," Bea points out. "And Mateo is, too. And Léo, don't forget."

"Who's Léo?" Annabelle asks.

"This really cute French guy—"

"Really cute," Bea interrupts.

"He was Hamlet in our spring play, and I was Ophelia. He's at Willow now."

Annabelle listens, nodding from time to time as I tell her about how I met Léo. She snorts when I get to the part about puking on him.

"How would it work out anyway, him being in France and me being here?" I say. "But still. It would have been nice to know him better."

"Has he reached out since closing night?" Bea asks.

"No, and I don't blame him. Who would want to be with a girl who threw up after she kissed him? And I don't want to text him. I don't want him to think I'm desperate."

"Maybe he's thinking the same," Annabelle puts in. "Maybe he thinks you don't like him."

I shake my head. "Guys don't think that way."

"Maybe *this* guy does, and you'll never know if you don't reach out. Why does saying what you feel make you look desperate?" She says this like she doesn't know the answer, either. "It's such a ridiculous standard." She kicks at a dandelion poking out of the gravel.

"Maybe you're right. Maybe French and British guys are different from Americans."

She snorts. "No."

"I wouldn't know what to say to Léo anyway. 'I didn't come to Willow because I'm pregnant'? That's not a good way to start a relationship."

"You're allowed to keep some things to yourself, you know. And besides, he'd be an asshat if he dumped you because of that."

"I know he'll understand," Bea adds. "He really is a good guy."

"I'm beginning to think good guys are the exception rather than the rule," Annabelle says.

Bea pushes her swing back. She drags her feet in the dusty hollow under the swing. "Was your guy nice, Camille? The one you . . ." She blushes.

"Dean?" I sit down in the swing next to her. "I wouldn't say he was nice like Léo's nice, but to be honest, he noticed me and that felt really special at the time. He had nice eyes and he didn't care what anyone thought about him, and I liked that." I twist in the swing and then let it go, spinning around in a circle.

"But, like, what was it like?" Bea asks.

"You really want to know?"

"Yeah," she says quietly, a little shy. "I really do."

TEN
APRIL

*D*ean was a regular at Iggy's, the ice cream shop I work at, which happens to be wedged between a strip joint and a truck stop. The strippers would come over, jeans pulled up over their sequined costumes, to buy chili cheese dogs and hot fudge sundaes, and the gas station guys would come over for extra-large root beer floats, and to flirt with the strippers.

Dean was one of those gas station guys. He was about eighteen and cute, with thick, dark hair that somehow managed to always look good, and the most unbelievable eyelashes I'd ever seen. The other Iggy's servers had determined that Dean was mine before I did and drifted away from the window whenever he came up, smelling faintly of diesel, his shirt half–tucked in. He'd smile as he picked up his milk shake, his hands rough and dirty with oil. He'd always order an extra puff of whipped cream and double rainbow sprinkles. The goofiness of that made my heart squeeze.

Two weeks of barbecue sandwiches and large vanilla milk shakes later, Dean asked me out. We went to a taco stand and ate burritos at a splintery picnic table. He told me about his family and how they liked to dress up as pioneers on the weekend and demonstrate frontier skills like whittling and hatchet throwing.

"I'd be happy to whittle you something," he said. "Do you like horses? I do a good horse."

"I love horses." I wasn't even sure what whittling was, but I didn't tell him that. I really wanted that horse.

"I'll do you a horse, then." He slid his legs out of the picnic table and went to the window, returning with another plate of tacos.

Two hours later, we were parked in the soccer field making out. We kissed until my lips were raw. He squeezed my breasts, lifting my bra from the bottom up, not bothering to try to undo the clasp.

"I have condoms," I whispered. Right after New Year's, I'd gotten it into my mind that I wanted to lose my virginity for no reason other than I wanted to feel more like an adult. I'd wanted to go on the pill, but I had to get a parent's permission to get it. So I ordered condoms from Amazon and hid them in an Altoids tin in my purse for whenever the chance might come along.

He pulled back and studied me for a moment. "Why would you carry condoms?"

"I thought, maybe, I should be ready." I realized how casual that sounded, like I'd be okay to have sex with any rando that happened to look my way. "I mean, in case you wanted to . . ." My voice trailed off. Maybe I shouldn't have mentioned the condoms. Maybe that was too much?

He leaned back in his seat and draped one arm over his steering wheel. "I never heard of a girl doing that. That's usually a dude thing, carrying condoms. A guy I know from work has a lucky condom." He grinned. "I think it's the same one he's had since middle school."

"Oh," I said because I didn't know what else to say.

"Can I see them?" He held out his hand.

I hesitated. "Why?"

He wiggled his fingers. "Come on."

I took a condom out of the Altoids tin and gave it to him. He took it, looked it over for a second, and then he handed it back to me.

"Did I buy the right ones?" I asked. "I mean, the right size or whatever?"

He didn't reply, but he did unzip his jeans. I reached for his T-shirt to take it off, because I thought you're supposed to be naked when you had sex. But he had other ideas. He pushed my hands away and left his shirt on.

I kicked my flip-flops off and wiggled out of my shorts and underwear, the condom clutched in my hand. The pleather seat burned hot against my bare skin. I wasn't sure if I was supposed to put the condom on him or if he would do it. But before I could ask, he grabbed it out of my hand. He pulled at the top with his fingers, but it didn't open. "Shit," he mumbled, then ripped the packet open with his teeth. I looked away while he put it on, and then he knelt between my legs.

I stared up at the roof; the material was torn at the corners and hung loose like polyester cobwebs. His truck smelled like grease and fried foods, the floor littered with bunched-up Iggy's bags. His NRA belt buckle lay across my underwear and shorts.

He buried his face in my neck. It felt awkward and smothering, like I was zipped all the way up in a sleeping bag.

I felt it bounce against my inner thigh but it didn't go in. I tilted my hips, hoping to get him pointed in the right direction, but that didn't seem to work, either. In the middle of all this, he looked up. "You're so soft," he said.

"Okay," I said.

He fumbled around a little more, and then I felt a pinch between my legs and Dean moved a little bit. "Yes!" he said. And then he groaned. And then it was over.

I don't know if he got all the way in, so I wasn't sure if I had lost my virginity or not.

Dean kind of just lay there on top of me, breathing heavily. To be honest, I really had no idea why he'd be so out of breath. Finally, he got up. He yanked off the condom and threw it out the window.

"Was that okay?" I asked. "We can try again." I started to pull my bra back down but I paused. "I mean, it was over kind of fast, so maybe—"

"Actually, I really need to get home." He started the truck.

I sat up and put my clothes back on, sliding one leg at a time into my underwear and then into my shorts.

He drove me back to Iggy's and pulled up to my car. The truck idled. He tapped his fingers on the steering wheel—drumming out the beat to a song we heard at the taco stand.

"Well, I guess I'll see you later?" I asked.

"Sure." He leaned over me and pulled the door handle. The door popped open, letting in a rush of hot air. I slid out and shut the door. I stood next to my car, watching as Dean's taillights faded into the night.

ELEVEN
JUNE 30

"That was the last I heard from Dean," I said. "He never came back to Iggy's ever. He never said goodbye. And I never got that whittled horse." I tried to laugh at this last part, but my breath caught instead.

"He sounds awful," Bea says.

"He sounds like he was a virgin," Annabelle says.

I turn my head and look at Annabelle, who is climbing the steps of the slide.

"What?" I say.

She slides down the short incline, her hands held out to the side. "He never had sex before, and he was embarrassed to tell you." She arrives at the bottom of the slide, her sneakers hitting the dirt. "That's why he struggled with the condom, that's why he couldn't get it in, that's why he didn't talk to you after. Total amateur hour. Guys don't know how to handle being a virgin. It's embarrassing for them. I mean, look how those dudes got upset when Bea embarrassed them."

"They ran us off the damn road," I say.

"Dudes don't have any scripts for how to fail. With women, there's no expectation we'll succeed so we know how to try again. Dudes ghost on you or get revenge."

"I never thought about it like that," I say.

"Not everything is about us. It's hard to know what he was thinking, but I wouldn't take it personally. Everyone has awkward sex." She smiles. "But also, don't let a guy tear the condom open with his teeth."

I let that truth sink in.

"How about you, Annabelle?" Bea asks.

"Bea! When did you get so interested in other people's sex lives?" I ask.

"Just because I don't have sex doesn't mean I'm not curious about it."

"I'll tell you about the first dick I ever touched. It belonged to a boy named Hayden. We went out freshman year." Annabelle sits on a pink spring horse, her sneakers flat on the ground.

"Oh my gosh! Freshman year?" Bea can't believe it.

"Hey! No judging. We used to make out in the little woods behind his house. He'd been not-so-subtly directing my hand toward his, you know, *stuff*, and one day, I was like, fine."

"What did you do?" Bea asks.

"I didn't know what to do," Annabelle says, "so I put it back where I found it."

Bea covers her mouth to suppress a laugh, which makes me burst out laughing. I like that about Annabelle, how open and honest she is.

"He wasn't too happy about that. So, I dumped him."

"What about you, Camille?" Annabelle says. "How was your first dick sighting?"

I shrug. "I've never actually had a sighting. It was dark when I did it with Dean, and he put the condom on himself."

"I've never seen one or felt a . . . *you know*," Bea says, bracing her feet against the ground, coming to a halt. "I mean, when Mateo and I make out, I feel a lump against me. But, like, I've never, you know, *touched* it."

I'm happy Bea is breaking out of her shell, but Mateo is like a brother to me, and the thought of him with a boner skeeves me out a little.

"I'm not sure I'd know what to do, much less how to put a condom on it," Bea says. "I wouldn't even know how to go about buying one."

"Whoa, good pony," Annabelle says to the spring horse, giving it a pat on the neck. She gets off. "Come on, women."

"Where're we going?" Bea asks.

"Shopping." She gestures at a drugstore down the street and takes off toward it. We exchange looks, get off the swings, and follow her.

"One of the benefits of working in a pharmacy is getting to stock all the crap," she says, opening the drugstore door. "I always stocked the personal items aisle because no one else wanted to do it."

Annabelle heads straight for one of the middle aisles and stops at the family planning section. The memory of the last time I was in this aisle flickers in my mind.

"I've never been down this aisle," Bea whispers, crowding close to me.

"Not even when you buy tampons?"

She shakes her head. "My mom buys them for me."

"Well, welcome to Thunderdome."

Annabelle stops in front of a rack of condoms. "And here we are, ladies. This is but a sampling of what awaits you in the world of condom usage." She crosses her arms and studies them. "Hmm, not a bad selection for such a Podunk pharmacy."

Bea keeps walking.

"Beatrice Delgado!" I say. "You get back over here. If I'm going to learn this, then you are, too."

"Yeah, Bea," Annabelle chimes in.

"All right!" she says. "Jeez Louise." She stands behind me, like the condoms might jump off the shelf and attack her.

"Now, listen carefully," Annabelle says. "Here on the left, you have your standard johnnies—"

"Johnnies?" I ask.

"Condoms are called johnnies in England—a little condom lingo I picked up. Please save your questions for the end of the lecture. Now, as I said." She points to each one. "As follows: Standards are for contraception and STD prevention only; no added features. Beginners should stick with these."

Annabelle goes on to explain size, reasons for lubrication, and latex versus polyurethane.

Bea shifts from foot to foot behind me, but she doesn't take off.

A girl looking at tampons down the aisle steps a little closer, her head cocked to one side, apparently listening.

"Here are the novelty condoms." Annabelle waves at the bottom shelf. "I suggest you consider these carefully because they are not always the best for protection. Know the difference." She takes a box off the shelf and holds it up. "Flavored condoms. Cherry." She puts it back and takes out another. "Grape. Artificially flavored. Perfect if you're on a diet."

The girl listening starts laughing.

"But seriously, you don't want sugar down there." Annabelle puts the box back on the shelf and chooses another. "Ribbed condoms. It says 'for her pleasure.'"

"That doesn't sound pleasurable," Bea says. "That sounds painful."

"Why do I want friction?" I ask.

"If a dude whips these out, run for the hills. Any guy who has to rely on a gimmick to do the job for him is just plain lazy." She scans the shelves. "Ah, here we have a glow-in-the-dark condom. Beloved of truck stop vending machines everywhere, these are for the bros in your life who want to see their dicks glow. Avoid, avoid."

"That would have been good for Dean," Bea whispers to me. "Then you would have seen it."

Annabelle continues. "Not illustrated here are warming condoms, colored condoms, and last but not least, your tingling condom."

"Tingling?" Bea asks.

"You ladies need help?" A clerk stands at the front of the aisle, confused.

Annabelle turns around, startled.

"Can I help you find something?" he asks.

Bea grabs a box of Trojans off the shelf. "Nope," she says. "We got it."

We run-walk to the cash register, trying desperately not to laugh. Bea steps to the cashier and drops the box of condoms on the counter like a boss.

We leave the shop and head back to the tire store. We're laughing so hard, we're weaving down the sidewalk.

"Oh my god, that poor guy," I say. "We must have looked crazy."

"What am I going to do with these condoms?" Bea says in a daze. "I can't believe I did that. I grabbed them off the shelf, and next thing you know, I bought them."

Annabelle puts her arm around Bea's shoulders. "That's our Bea!"

At six thirty, Dale comes into the customer room. "Car's out front, girls," he says around his toothpick. "Y'all be careful now." He hands Annabelle the keys.

We get in Buzzi, and Annabelle turns on the radio. Bea opens her pack of condoms, and they furl out in a long strip. She tears one off, takes the condom out, and unrolls it. "Interesting," she whispers.

"So how do these go on, Annabelle?" Bea asks as we pull onto the freeway. "Is it, like, self-explanatory?"

"Nope," she says. "I had to look on the internet for instructions."

"Planned Parenthood website says . . ." Bea's voice fades as she reads. "Gosh . . . hmm . . . okay." I hear her phone click off.

"Come on!" Annabelle says. "Keep reading. Don't leave us in suspense here."

"No, I'm good," Bea says firmly. "I know how now."

"You read it, Camille," Annabelle says.

"On it." I look up the Planned Parenthood website on my phone and click on *contraception*. There's a step-by-step chart, complete with line drawings of condoms and a naked dude. "Okay, so in a nutshell—"

Bea and Annabelle burst into laughter.

"Nutshell!" Bea says through giggles.

"Hush, you two," I say. "This is important, so listen. Basically you wait to put the condom on until the guy has an erection."

"That makes sense," Annabelle says.

"Also you should check the expiration date—"

"Of the guy's dick?"

I throw Annabelle a withering look. "No, genius. The condoms! Moving along." I read the next part, and I start laughing so hard, I can't stop. "I can't . . ." I can barely get the words out.

"What?" Annabelle says.

"I know why she's laughing," Bea says.

"Why?"

"The end should look like a little hat," Bea says.

"What?" Annabelle says.

"That way you know you've got it the right way around."

"Brilliant," Annabelle says. "That's seared into my brain forever now."

I get hold of myself and continue. "Next, you're supposed to pinch the tip and put it on the end of your penis," I say.

"Got it, got it," Annabelle says, nodding. "End of my penis."

"The pictures are something else," Bea says.

"Then roll it down, stop when you reach the base. God, I'm glad I don't have a dick," I say.

"Don't feel too sorry for dudes," Annabelle says. "Putting on a condom is about the hardest thing they have to do with those things. That and getting kicked in the nuts."

"It hurts to get kicked in the vagina, too," I say. "I fell on the bar of my bike when I was ten and it hurt so bad. My mom traded it in for a girl's bike after that. I guess it was okay for my brother, Chris, to fall on it."

Bea snorts.

"So go on," Annabelle says. "This is fascinating."

"I thought you knew how to do this?"

"It's always good to have a refresher."

"Next up, it says have sex—"

"Duh," Bea says.

"Then take it off before your penis goes soft," I read. "Make sure to hold the end of the condom when you do this. Pull it off from the tip and discard." I start laughing again. "It says not to throw it in the toilet because it clogs the pipes."

"Can you imagine telling your parents you've clogged the toilet with used condoms?" Annabelle says. "Mortifying."

"My parents would send me to a convent if that happened," Bea says.

I click off my phone. "So now we know the ins and outs of condoms."

Bea and Annabelle erupt in hysterics.

"What?"

"Nutshell. Ins and outs," Bea says between giggles. A packaged condom flies through the air and lands on my lap. "Here. You win the condom award."

I pick up the condom and pretend to sob in joy. "I'd like to thank the Academy and all the boys in the world who have to turn their dicks into balloon animals to do it."

"You've earned it, Camille," Annabelle says.

"I have my own lucky condom now," I say.

We drive for a little while, listening to an interview show on public radio.

"What's our ETA?" Annabelle asks.

I look at the Maps app. "Eleven if we don't stop for bathroom breaks."

"Or coffee." Bea taps the back of Annabelle's head.

Annabelle grips the wheel and sighs. "It feels good to be finally on our way."

Bea leans forward and hooks her elbows over the seat. "Shall I call around to see if we can get a hotel room in Alamo?"

"We already have one," Annabelle says. "Camille needs to rest after she takes the pills, and we wanted to make sure we had a room ready."

"Why? Can't you rest on the way home, Camille?" Bea asks.

Annabelle looks at me.

"No," I say slowly. "I need to be near a toilet because . . . because." I try to reach for words that Bea will understand. Words that won't upset her.

"It will be like a miscarriage, Bea," Annabelle puts in. She says it gently, looking in her rearview mirror at her.

"Oh," Bea says. "I didn't think about that. I don't know what I thought . . . that maybe the pills would make it dissolve or something. That's so dumb of me."

"You couldn't have known," I say. "And why would you? I didn't really know about any of this until I needed to."

"Will it hurt?"

"It's supposed to feel like a really bad period . . . so"—I shrug—"I have ibuprofen, and I brought my heating pad with me."

"How big will it be?" she asks.

"Will what be?" I ask.

"The . . . you know."

"Don't think about it, Bea—" Annabelle says.

"I'm eleven weeks pregnant so it's about an inch and a half," I interrupt. I hold my thumb and forefinger up. "About this big."

Annabelle glances at me, shakes her head.

"She asked, and so I'm going to tell her," I say. I know why Bea's asking, because she's like me. There's something about knowing what's going to happen and how it's going to happen that's calming. When I'm at the dentist, I ask exactly how long I'll be stuck in that chair with my mouth wide open. When my grandma went into the nursing home, I wanted to know why, and I made my parents tell me everything.

"Will you see it . . . floating in the toilet?" Bea asks.

"I don't know what I'll be able to see. I might see a little sack and maybe even the fetus," I say.

"Okay," Bea says quietly. "What will you do after it comes out? Flush it down the toilet?"

"Yes."

Bea doesn't say anything more, and I don't press her to talk.

"What sort of plays did you do in England?" I ask Annabelle. We're flying down the highway, making good time.

"Let's see. We did *King Lear* and *Waiting for Godot*."

"Ugh," I say. "I hate that play."

"Yeah, it wasn't my favorite, but the creative director has a thing for Beckett, which I don't understand because she's a woman and Beckett hated women."

"Tracy despised him. That famous 'women have no prostates' excuse and that's why they can't play the male characters is beyond."

Annabelle shifts the car and changes lanes.

"Do you like England?"

"I do. It's expensive, though, although I found this café where you can get curry and rice for four pounds. But curry and rice gets old after a while."

I imagine Annabelle riding the Tube, getting off at Piccadilly station or whatever it's called, and walking around London past Buckingham Palace and Scotland Yard and Big Ben, a cute scarf wrapped around her neck, umbrella hooked over her arm. "Did you go to Stratford-upon-Avon?"

She shakes her head.

"Did you meet any guys there? I love accents, especially French and British—"

"I don't really want to talk about England anymore, okay?" Annabelle says. She looks a little upset.

"Oh, okay," I say, dropping the subject.

"Camille," Bea says, "you never told me how you and Annabelle met up." Bea has always been good about redirecting a conversation.

"Annabelle was home for summer break working at that pharmacy off the freeway."

"Fred's Pharmacy?" Bea says. "Ugh, that place is so gross."

"Yeah, no joke. I didn't stay long," Annabelle says. "God, I was so freaked out when I saw you, Camille."

I laugh. "I was freaked out when I saw *you*! I mean, I was your biggest fan, and no way did I want you to see me buying a pregnancy test."

TWELVE
JUNE 22

The orange neon sign for Fred's Pharmacy stutters on and off; the top part of the *F* is burned out. A plastic grocery bag dangles from a lamppost, and Sonic cups stabbed with straws lie scattered under the parking lot lights, their contents sucked dry long ago.

The clock in my mom's old Buick ticks as the second hand sweeps around once, then again and again.

I stare at my hands, begging them to let go of the damn steering wheel. But I sit here, seat belt clicked in place; my hands stuck to the faux leather like a bird clutching its perch.

My phone dings in my purse, shaking me out of my zombie state. I scramble through my bag to find it. A text message from my mom:

Where are you? Who said you could take the car?

Shit. I open the door and a rush of hot air blasts in. My phone dings again.

You'd better be on your way home.

I didn't expect to be gone this long. I saw someone I knew in the pharmacy at Bridgetown and so I drove to this drugstore, which is a half hour away from my house. I've never taken my mom's car without permission before and never driven it this far, but I didn't know what else to do. I thought she'd still be at church with my dad.

I shove my phone in my back pocket, cringing at the ding that follows. I can almost feel my mom's anger radiating hot through the screen. I run-walk across the parking lot.

I rummage in my purse for my sunglasses and slide them on. Sunnies aren't much of a disguise, but it makes me feel a little better. The automatic doors slide open.

I search for the sign marked FEMININE NEEDS and force my feet in that direction, taking a shortcut down the INFANT NEEDS aisle. The only person there is an employee tagging baby formulas.

My sneakers squeak to a stop on the scuffed tile floor. I know that employee.

What the hell is Annabelle Ponsonby doing here?

Annabelle sports a tomato-red vest with HOW MAY I HELP YOU? written on the back in peeling iron-on letters. I have to get out of here, find another pharmacy. No way can Annabelle Ponsonby see me buying a pregnancy test. I step away, and a loud *ding!* comes from my pocket. Annabelle glances over. I think her eyes light up when she sees me, but then her face instantly falls.

"Hey, Annabelle," I say. "I thought that was you. Um. Aren't you supposed to be in England?"

She goes back to tagging the formula.

"I'm home for the summer," she says. *Click, click, click.*

Go! Go now! Find another drugstore. "Oh, that makes sense. I was in the neighborhood, and I got thirsty, so I thought, you know, I'd get something to, uh, deal with that. The thirst."

"Aisle one."

"Cool, thanks." I walk away from her toward aisle one, just in case Annabelle is watching, and pull my phone from my pocket. *WHERE ARE YOU?*

I look over my shoulder at Annabelle, who's gone back to tagging.

"Hey, Annabelle." A skinny guy with neck acne wanders down the aisle toward her. "The toilet overflowed in the bathroom."

"So clean it up," she snaps.

"Not me, dude. You're on bathroom duty."

Annabelle shoves the tagger into the guy's hands and heads off, disappearing through a pair of swinging doors at the back of the store.

I make a U-turn to the feminine needs aisle. *Just grab it and go!* My heart is pounding, sweat starting to pool in my armpits.

Tampons, personal lubrication, feminine wash, ovulation kits . . . Where are the pregnancy tests? I start at the beginning of the aisle again and stare the shelves up and down. Finally I find them tucked on top of the last shelf next to a dusty display of women-only vitamins and locked in a plastic box. *PLEASE SEE AN ASSOCIATE FOR ASSISTANCE*, a label on the box reads.

Ding!

CAMILLE. WHERE. ARE. YOU?

I race to the checkout, and I get in line behind a woman buying six gallons of milk. There's a candy rack nearby. I reach for a king-sized Hershey's bar with almonds. I notice a stack of Altoids in the rack next to the chocolates. My stomach twists at the sight of the black lettering scribbled across the cheerful red-and-white tin boxes.

The woman begins to argue with the cashier about her coupon.

A man moves in behind me and stands so close, I can smell his breath: Beer Nuts and bourbon. I step forward and hold my breath, closing my eyes a little. The woman storms off, leaving the six milks on the counter.

The cashier sighs. She's maybe in her seventies with gray hair permed into tight curls. The perm must have been recent, judging from the ammonia scent wafting off her head. "Next," she says, reaching over the milks for my chocolate bar. She smiles. "Oh, that used to be my favorite, darlin', but I can't eat it anymore. The almonds get stuck in my bridge."

"Yeah, me too. Um . . . I need some help with one of the products, ma'am," I say, lowering my voice. "The pregnancy tests are locked up."

"The whats, honey?" she says, her fingers pausing over the register. "You'll have to speak up, I'm a little hard of hearing."

I clear my throat and lean forward. "The pregnancy tests, ma'am. They are, uh, locked in a box?"

"Oh, those are locked up because they get stolen a lot." She sets the chocolate bar on the counter. "You'll have to talk to the pharmacist."

The man behind me grumbles under his breath.

"Oh, okay," I say, trying to sound like it's no big deal.

"Do you still want that candy bar?"

The guy reaches around me and tosses a Slim Jim on the counter. The bright red stick spins to a stop against the six milk jugs.

I shake my head and walk to the back of the store to the pharmacist's counter. There is a long line of people waiting to pick up their prescriptions, and I get in behind them. I hitch my bag over my shoulder and pretend to be interested in the nail polish display. The pink, green, blue, and gold colors blur into a rainbow through my sudden tears. I shove the sunglasses onto my head and rub dry my eyes with the palms of my hands.

Finally, it's my turn.

"Next," he says. He shoves a pen into the pocket on his white medical coat. The top of the pocket is dotted with blue ink stains.

My cheeks instantly start to burn. "Um. I need a pregnancy test." I wave my hand toward the feminine needs aisle. "You have them locked up down there."

He frowns so hard that the furrows on his brow squash together. "Is this for you?"

"Does it matter?"

"Are you married?"

"No."

"How old are you?" he asks, and not very nicely.

"I'm, um, seventeen."

He draws his head back. "Seventeen? You're seventeen and you're asking for a pregnancy test?" He tuts.

I don't say a word.

"You haven't been treating your body well, young lady, if it's a pregnancy test you're after. You know, the more boys you allow to have their way with you, the less you'll have to offer your husband. No one wants a piece of chewed-up gum, now do they?"

I feel tears prickling at my eyes again. I don't want him to see me cry. But it's too late.

"Can you just—"

"Do your parents know what you're up to?"

"No," I say. "I mean . . ." I don't know what to say now.

"Go on home and talk to your parents. My conscience won't let me sell something like that to you without their knowing. I'm a father myself, and I wouldn't like it if my daughter could buy pregnancy tests or contraception or anything else like that without my knowledge."

I see people looking at me, watching the show. I step back against the shelves, as if the bottles of vitamins and pain relievers will protect me from their stares.

The pharmacist rubs his chin; I hear the scratching of his stubble under his hand.

A man behind me pipes up. "When I was your age, young lady, girls used aspirin as birth control. Hold an aspirin between your legs and you'll never get pregnant."

My tears are falling now, fast and heavy. I duck my head and turn to leave.

And there stands Annabelle Ponsonby, a mop and bucket in her hand, watching me with a look of shock on her face.

I bolt for the car.

I lay my forehead on the steering wheel. *What now?*

I hold my hand flat against my stomach. What is going on in there? I can almost feel cells dividing. An image of me pregnant flashes into my head. My stomach poking out while everyone else heads off to begin their lives. I think about my parents helping me raise a baby, and I can barely breathe.

No. That won't happen. I can't let it happen.

I sit with my head against the steering wheel, when a tap on the window makes me jump. I look up to see Annabelle, gesturing for me to roll the window down.

I start the car and hit the window button. "Annabelle," I say. "What—"

"Here," she says. She tosses something through the window. First Response pregnancy test.

Annabelle turns and trudges across the parking lot, pulling off her smock as she goes. She drops it on the ground and kicks it. She flips the building the bird and then climbs into a beat-up Ford Focus. I watch as she screeches out of the parking lot, barely pausing at the stop sign and disappearing around the corner.

My phone starts to ring. *Mom* lights up the screen. I don't answer it. I shove the box and my phone in my purse, start the car, and drive home, staring at the road through a waterfall of tears.

THIRTEEN
JUNE 30

"I am so glad I quit that night," Annabelle says.

"That's why you flipped the building the bird?" I ask.

She grins. "Oh, you saw that."

"I saw you kick your apron, too. That was pretty classy, I have to say."

"I'm all about the class."

"I'm really sorry, Camille," Bea says. "The pharmacist shouldn't have treated you that way."

"Well, dudes like that are, for the most part, jerks," Annabelle responds. "Can you imagine how entitled you must be to spew out that crap to someone? I can't imagine telling a girl she's a chewed-up piece of gum. I couldn't tell my worst enemy that."

"Don't let him hurt your feelings, Camille," Bea says.

"It's hard not to. He basically slut-shamed me, and right in front of the whole place."

"That was his plan," Annabelle puts in. "Public shaming. If he could have come out with a scarlet *S*, he would have. Stick you in the stocks and have people pelt rotten tomatoes at you."

"You remember what Mr. Knight says when we get bad reviews?" Bea asks.

"Don't take them personally." All three of us say it together.

From the back seat, Bea pats my shoulder. "That jerk probably says that garbage to every woman who comes into that pharmacy, no matter how old she is."

I can't help but smile a little when Bea says that.

"Bea's right," Annabelle says. "Like bad reviews, that kind of thing can burrow its way into your head and you can't get rid of it, you know?"

"But that day is like a movie in my mind that I can turn on and torture myself with."

"Tammy told me to kick the dust off my feet and forget about those boys," Bea says. "You do that, too, Camille. Kick the dust off your feet and forget about that pharmacist."

"He didn't win anyway," I say. "I got the test, thanks to Annabelle."

"What was it like, taking that test?" Bea asks. "I mean, was it like in *Juno*?"

"Yep, Camille drank all the SunnyD she could find," Annabelle says.

I nudge her with my elbow.

"How do those tests even work?" Bea asks. "I mean, how can a stick say whether you're pregnant or not? Wouldn't it have been better to go to a doctor?"

Annabelle holds up her hand. "Really, Bea? Like what doctor?" she says.

Bea sits back in her seat and huffs.

"I had myself convinced that the test would say *not pregnant*, and this entire nightmare would be over. I could go to Willow, get Léo to fall in love with me, forget this ever happened." My stomach pitches and nausea rolls over me at even the thought of it.

"But what happened?" Bea asks.

I look back at her, and she has this really earnest expression on her face. "So, my mom is pissed because I took the car without her permission. She has all these people over, and she punishes me by making me work the party. I have to wait for a moment when she's not having me, like, fill up someone's drink or bring out another tray of cheese. But finally, she releases me, and I race upstairs to the bathroom." I remember how my heart pounded as I walked up the stairs.

"And?" Bea is leaning forward in her seat.

"Well, I take out the test and read the instructions, and then I sit on the toilet." I pause, reliving the moment. "And all that's going through my mind is, like, *Please don't be pregnant, please don't be pregnant*. You know?"

Annabelle nods, but she doesn't take her eyes off the road.

"I'm sitting there, and I wait and wait, but I can't go. I turn on the sink and hold my hand in the water for a solid minute. But it doesn't work."

"So, the exact opposite of who you've been this whole car ride?" Annabelle asks.

"Yes," I say, shoving her gently. "I put the test back in the box and start guzzling water from the sink. Downstairs, my mom's party is in full swing, and I hear one of the ladies scream out, '*Bunco!*'"

"What the hell is Bunco?" Annabelle asks.

"Oh my gosh, it's so fun!" Bea replies. "We'll teach you later. Camille, please go on."

"So, finally, I feel like I have to pee. And this shot of fear pulses through me."

Annabelle reaches over and squeezes my leg.

"I sit on the toilet and I put the stick under me, and this time a trickle of pee comes out. I'm not sure if it's enough, or if it even hits the stick, but it looks damp when I pull it out. I put the stick on a piece of toilet paper on the sink and set the timer on my phone for three minutes. Which feels like forever, and you'll recall, way longer than the sex I had. And I'm sitting there, wondering why the hell I even had sex with Dean. I was just so eager to lose my virginity, to have 'the experience,' to add it to my arsenal as an actress. To, I don't know, *be a woman*."

"I get that," Annabelle says. "That's how I felt when I did it for the first time."

"I didn't even consider the possibility I could get pregnant. I thought condoms were foolproof, you know?"

I look out the window at the streetlights zipping by.

"So then what happened?" Bea says it all quiet.

"The timer went off." I grimace at the memory. "And there were two pink lines on the little screen."

"What do two pink lines mean?"

"Jesus, Bea!" Annabelle says. "It meant that she was pregnant."

"I was pregnant," I say kind of softly to myself. The words still feel weird coming out of my mouth. A hush falls over the car.

"Bunco!" Annabelle suddenly shouts, startling the shit out of me. Bea actually screams.

Even though I find Annabelle's behavior less than funny, her grin *is* a bit contagious.

FOURTEEN

*W*e drive in silence for what feels like an eternity. Bea falls
asleep in the back seat. The radio gets staticky, and Annabelle
turns it off. The sudden silence confuses me. The day has been so
loud, so active. I wonder what everyone else is doing; I wonder if
there are any posts from the kids at Willow. I look at my phone,
my thumb hovering on the Instagram app.

"Don't do it," Annabelle says, shooting a look at me. "That
way lie dragons, and I'm not kidding."

"I just wanted to—"

"Yeah, well, maybe you just wanted to, but I'm telling you that
you'll drop down a hole of suck you won't be able to crawl out of."

Annabelle is right. Seeing pics of Willow, especially selfies
from the kids from the Globe, would end me.

Instead, I text my mom to tell her I'm still alive. She replies with a thumbs-up, which suits me fine.

Around ten or so, Annabelle yawns.

"Do you want to stop for coffee?" I ask.

She grips the wheel, blinking. "No, I don't want to waste more time. I'm okay."

"You sure? I mean, you're basically fueled by the stuff."

She looks in the side mirror and changes lanes. "I'm fine."

I go back to playing Candy Crush. Two seconds later the car weaves to the right, almost into the other lane. A car honks, swerving away from Buzzi. Annabelle's eyes are half-closed.

"Annabelle!" I shove her.

She opens her eyes and jerks the car back on the road. "Shit!"

Bea wakes up. "What's going on?"

"That was close," I say. Adrenaline is pumping through my body. "We nearly hit that car."

"We'd better stop somewhere," Annabelle says. She leans forward over the steering wheel, staring at the road, shaking her head and blinking.

"On it," Bea says.

I look at Maps to see what hotels and motels are near. There are four. Bea and I split the calls between us.

"All booked up," I say.

"Same," Bea says. "What now?"

"I don't think I can keep driving anymore," Annabelle says. "I think we'll have to find a parking lot and sleep in the car."

"Okay," I say slowly, not loving that idea at all.

Bea hooks her elbows over the seat. "Sleeping in the car is

dangerous. I've listened to enough true-crime podcasts to know. The *Murder and Mayhem* girls talk about that all the time."

"I just need, like, twenty minutes to rest," Annabelle says curtly. "I'm sure we won't get killed in twenty minutes."

Bea doesn't stop talking. "Some creep will attack us while we're sleeping. Think of those stories about serial murderers getting people in their cars. What about that killer's hook dangling from those people's car handle?"

"You can stay awake and watch for monsters, how about that?" Annabelle snaps.

"I think you should stop listening to the *Murder and Mayhem* girls," I say. I twist around in my seat and give her a look that tells her to shut up because she's freaking out Annabelle. "That hook thing is an urban myth."

"Hey, I learn a lot on that podcast."

"Walmarts let you park overnight," I say.

"I don't know," Annabelle says. "I'm not thrilled with the idea of parking next to other people. Seems like prime creep territory to me."

"Ted Bundy picked up girls in his Volkswagen," Bea says, continuing with her ghoulish comments. "He was handsome and charming and girls got right in his car, no questions. He murdered every single one of them."

"We're not getting in anyone's car!" Annabelle screeches.

"Jeez, Bea!" I say. "Seriously."

"I'm just sayin'," Bea mumbles.

Annabelle takes the next exit and into a town that's seen better days. It's a ghost town. There's a twenty-four-hour fish fry restaurant with a lit parking lot, but we pass by because a bunch of guys are hanging out front. Same with the two-pump gas station and the Cigs and Smokes shop.

"Jesus," Annabelle says. "Those guys look like they're up to no good."

"Yeah," I say.

Bea sinks lower in her seat.

Annabelle slows down in front of a janky, boarded-up strip club. A burned-out neon sign hangs over the door that says THE BOOBIE BUNGALOW. The Os are painted in with pink breasts.

She gives me a long look and I shrug.

"The Boobie Bungalow it is, then."

From the back seat, Bea whimpers.

We drive into the cracked parking lot as close to the Boobie Bungalow as we can, as if it could protect us. We lock all the doors.

"The Boobie Bungalow?" Bea says. "Are they serious right now?"

"That's the most original name I have ever heard for a strip joint," Annabelle says, studying the sign. "Gotta give them credit for that one."

"Gets right to the point, for sure," I say.

"There's one in England called the Cinnamon Tortoise," she says. "That's really reaching, if you ask me. I suppose all the good names were taken."

"What would you call a strip club?" I ask. "I mean, if you owned one."

She thinks. "How about the Man Cave?"

"The Landing Strip?" I say, and Annabelle laughs.

"The Jug Hut?"

"The Panty Palace?" I offer.

"Nice one," Annabelle says.

"I know some strippers, and they make good money. There's a strip club down the street from Iggy's where I work. They come over on their break all the time, and they are so nice. They club together at Christmastime and buy us all little boxes of Whitman's Samplers and tie them with glittery red bows. There's one girl called Ruby Tuesday who always buys a Diet Coke float. She's my favorite. She told me she made enough money to pay rent and all her bills with enough left over to pay for her kids' activities."

"Would you ever do it? Be a stripper, I mean?" Annabelle asks.

"I'm not a good enough dancer," I say. "No one would hire me. I took a pole dancing class once and left with a ton of bruises."

"What makes me laugh is all those asshat guys who clack about women cockteasers and how shitty they are," Annabelle says. "And then they go to a strip club and pay women to cocktease them."

"I wonder why the Boobie Bungalow closed down," I say. "If a strip joint can't make it in a town, what can?" I got worried for the strippers then, picturing someone like Ruby Tuesday losing her job and having to find another in a town that couldn't support a strip joint. A job that paid enough so her kids could keep their activities.

"I don't know," she says. She gives the Boobie Bungalow a long look, then pulls her hoodie over her head and falls asleep in two seconds.

I thought Bea had fallen asleep while Annabelle and I were talking. But the back door opens, and Bea gets out. She slams the door harder than the door requires and walks over to the Boobie Bungalow. She stares at it for a long while and then starts walking away, her arms crossed over her chest.

I get out of the car. "Hey!"

Bea ignores me and starts hurrying like she's got someplace to be.

I follow. "Bea! Get back here. It's not safe to go wandering around like that. Remember the guy with the hook hand?"

"I don't care," she tosses over her shoulder. "Go back to the car and leave me alone."

"Where are you going?"

"Far away from you and Annabelle, your new bestie."

"Hey!" I reach her and grab her shoulder. "What does that mean?" Bea shrugs, but I hang on and make her stop. "Annabelle is not my bestie, okay?"

"She is too!"

"I don't know why you're saying that. I barely know her."

"Oh, come on, Camille. You two have so much more in common than we do now. You can laugh and talk about strip joints and sex and . . . stuff."

"What stuff?"

"And when did you take a pole dancing class?"

"I—"

"I have exactly zero to add to that conversation." She holds her fingers in a little *O.* "Zero."

"You do, too, Bea. You've been holding your own in every conversation we've been having," I point out.

"I don't understand half of what you're saying."

"Is this about the abortion pill? About the fetus? I'm sorry, Bea, I shouldn't have told you. Annabelle thought you'd be upset—"

Bea flings her arms up. "See! Let's not upset Bea! When did you ever worry about upsetting me?"

"Because I would never talk about this stuff in front of you, ever! I know it makes you uncomfortable, and I don't want to do that."

"I'm tired of you protecting me. Of keeping things from me. Just like my parents do, and I'm sick of it. I never thought you'd treat me that way, like they do. Like I'm some delicate flower or something."

"I'm sorry—"

"We tell each other everything, Camille, and you know it. You never told me about that Dean guy. You had a crush on a guy, and you had s-sex," Bea stumbles over the word. "You did it with him, and you never said anything to me!"

"We don't talk about things like that," I say. "What was I supposed to tell you? 'Oh, hey, Bea, FYI, while you were training to be a teen youth minister, I had awkward sex with a guy in a soccer field who ghosted on me the second he put his pants back on'?"

Bea crosses her arms again and looks away, her jaw set. "You should've told me."

"What good would that have done? I told you about being pregnant pretty much right away and look how you treated me."

"I didn't do that to be mean to you. I thought I was doing what was best for you." Bea grows quiet. "That was a mistake, and I realized it when I saw you sitting there in the Holler Up with Annabelle. At first I was really jealous because you were sitting in our booth, and you were with someone way, way cooler than me. But then, after you told me she was going to drive you, I knew it was my fault you were there with her. I let you down."

Bea starts crying.

FIFTEEN

JUNE 27

Everyone is at work, and I have the house to myself, which is good. I sit in my bedroom researching on my laptop. Each time I think I understand Texas abortion restrictions, another page says something contradictory, and it seems to be changing by the day. What was true a few years ago is different now. I don't know. I shut my laptop.

This much is clear: I can't get an abortion through a clinic—that's completely out of the running. I pull up the Greyhound bus schedule. It takes at least eight hours by bus to get to the border. I look up hotels near there. The cheapest I find is sixty bucks a night.

Okay, this is good. I got this.

But I don't got this, because the website says I need someone I trust to stay with me as the tissue passes. I can grit my way through it. But what if that's not enough? How much pain and blood is too much before I know I need a hospital? I picture myself on the floor of some janky hotel by the border, all alone, bleeding to death.

What is wrong with me? Why don't I have more friends in my life I can trust with anything? All my friends come from the Globe, and we only have acting in common. I've spent my whole life in a mini-clique with Bea, creating our own little world. We shared Harry Potter, model horses, camp, Shakespeare, Oreos, problems with our parents. We were always in lockstep, always in full agreement. But now all that's gone.

I have no one to sit with me. No one.

And then Annabelle Ponsonby pops into my mind. Someone willing to buy a twenty-five-dollar test for a girl she barely knows would probably be trustworthy. But what would I say to her? "Hey, we were in a couple of plays together. Would you mind driving me to Mexico to get an abortion?"

But I am out of options, so I look on the Globe directory for Annabelle's number. I cringe as I tap in each digit.

There are a few seconds of silence before someone speaks: "Hello?" It's Annabelle, and she doesn't sound friendly.

I'm about to say sorry, wrong number, and hang up the phone, but I wade in. "Um . . . sorry, this is Camille? Camille Winchester?"

"Oh, hey, Camille. Sorry about the crap hello. What's up?"

"I'm sorry I didn't contact you earlier. About the pregnancy test?"

"What about it?"

"To thank you. And I need to pay you. My mind has been in a tailspin for the past few days, to be honest."

"Hey, no problem, and you don't owe me anything. I'm sorry that pharmacist was such a dick. Is everything okay?"

The worst she can say is no.

"Not really. I'm pregnant," I whisper, bracing myself for her reaction.

"Fuck."

"I can't find a way to get a legal abortion."

"Meet me at the Holler Up in fifteen minutes."

Annabelle sits across from me in a booth at the Holler Up. When she picks up her coffee cup, I see that her fingernails are bitten down as far as a person can bite without hitting skin.

The restaurant is decorated for the Fourth of July. Cardboard flags are taped all over the walls. An exploding shower of red, white, and blue fireworks dot each corner of our paper placemats, and a bowl of candies wrapped in plastic flags sit next to a basket of packaged oyster crackers.

Our waitress comes by and refills Annabelle's coffee and drops another Sprite for me. Someone behind me ordered a patty melt, and the smell of fried onions, something I used to love, makes me want to hurl. I grab a pack of oyster crackers and tear them open. I feel so tired, I want to put my head down on the table and take a nap.

"I don't know all that much about buying abortion pills," Annabelle says, "but I know it's something people do. I read an article about it after the clinics closed down."

"Is it legal, though? If something goes wrong . . . can I go to jail?"

Annabelle shrugs. "I don't know, but is it worth it to you to risk it?"

I wrap my hands around my soda, pressing my fingers against the cold plastic. "I want an abortion. I'm going to do this. I can take a bus to Hidalgo and—"

"You don't have to take a bus. I'll take you."

"Why?" I've had more lines in a play with Annabelle than I've had actual conversations, and yet she's offering to take me hours away to get an abortion pill.

She leans forward. "If you have to go all the way to the border, then I will take you. Gladly."

"Why would you do this for me?" I ask.

"Because I would hope my friends would do it for me. We can drive there in my car, get the pills at that flea market, and come back when it's done," Annabelle says.

"What if they don't have it? What then?"

"We'll go to Mexico. Do you have a passport?"

"Yeah." My family all got passports for a trip we planned to take to Mexico last year, but we didn't end up going. "I'll pay for everything," I put in quickly.

"I'll take care of food. It won't be much. We can go tomorrow if you want to." She reaches over and takes a pack of oyster crackers.

"Actually, could we leave Monday?"

"Sure, no sweat."

Finally, a plan, a certainty. A way to make this all go away, with someone who understands. Someone who doesn't judge.

"When do you go back to England?" I ask.

"Sorry?" she says over the rattle of the cellophane packet.

"England?"

"End of summer." She crunches into a cracker.

"I bet you can't wait to leave."

She shrugs, her mouth full of crackers.

"Were you homesick when you first left?" As much as I'm ready to leave Johnson Creek, the thought of being far away from home makes me apprehensive.

She gives me the side-eye. "Hardly." She reaches for another pack of crackers. "So who is the guy? Does he know? If you don't mind me asking, I mean."

"I . . . um, no. I only went out with him a couple times." I pick up my straw wrapper and wind it around my finger. "Don't tell anyone, would you?"

She shrugs. "Who would I tell? It's none of my business what you do with your body."

"Bea would not agree with you."

"Bea Delgado?"

"Yeah. She's my best friend. Or, I guess, *was* my best friend."

"Wait a second. Did Bea break up with you because of this?" Annabelle gets really pissed again. "I hate girls like that, seriously. I'm so glad to be out of Johnson Creek High School, home of the virgin princesses. What the fuck business is it of hers? I mean, how does this impact her life?" She leans back in the booth, crossing her arms.

Part of me is glad Annabelle is on my side, but another part hates to hear someone bad-mouth my best friend.

"I get what you're saying . . ."

"Ditch girls like that, I mean it. Those slut-shaming girls are beyond."

"I guess I never thought of her like that."

"Well, have a thought."

The busboy comes by holding a plastic tub of dirty dishes and eyes our table, moving on when both of us grab our cups.

I can't believe this is the first real conversation I've ever had with Annabelle Ponsonby. Instead of talking about acting and what she's learning in England, we're talking about do-it-yourself abortions and how crappy people are, particularly my best friend. This truly and completely sucks. The song "God Bless the USA" starts to play. The corny lyrics and the sappy way the guy sings them remind me of that abortion parental-bypass judge I saw this morning. I bet he loves this song. I bet his barbershop quartet is planning on singing it at some patriotic Fourth of July event.

I start to tell Annabelle about him, but she's looking over my shoulder. "Speak of the devil." She points with her chin. "Bea just walked in with some dude."

I slink down in my booth a little. "Of course."

"They're coming this way."

I glance over my shoulder; the two of them are making a bee-line straight for our table.

"Camille?" Bea says. "I thought that was you."

"Hey, Cam," Mateo says. "Haven't seen you for a while. Sorry about Willow." His eyes dart around. "That sucks."

"Why haven't you replied to any of my texts?" Bea asks.

Bea finally notices Annabelle. She does a double take, her

expression turning from fangirl admiration to confusion in two seconds. It would be funny if this whole thing weren't so awful.

"Whoa, Annabelle Ponsonby," Mateo says under his breath.

"Annabelle? What are you doing here?" Bea asks.

Annabelle lifts her coffee cup and widens her eyes. "I am drinking coffee." Every word drips with sarcasm, which I know will hurt Bea's feelings. I should say something to make it less hurtful, but I can't. I feel caught. I want to crawl under the booth.

Bea's jaw twists, and she looks at Mateo.

Annabelle's phone buzzes in her pocket, and she takes it out and glances at it. "I gotta bounce. You want a ride home?"

"That's okay. I'm going to sit here for a little bit. I'll walk home."

"You sure?"

I nod.

"I'll see you Monday then, okay?"

Bea watches Annabelle walk away, and then she turns to me. "Why are you talking to Annabelle Ponsonby, and what's Monday?"

"None of your business."

"I, uh . . . ," Mateo says, slowly backing away from the booth. "I'm gonna go sit at the counter and grab a cheeseburger."

Bea slides into the booth.

"What do you want, Bea?"

"I want to know what's going on with you. I'm worried."

"You are not. Save it."

"I care about you, and you know I do."

"Okay, so do you care that I have to go all the way to the border to buy pills?"

Bea levels a look at me. "Is Annabelle Ponsonby going with you?"

"Yes, she is. She's actually driving me. I barely know her and she's being a better friend than you." I want to hurt her as badly as she hurt me. And now I don't care that Annabelle hurt her damn feelings.

Bea's face flushes. She doesn't say another word. She gets up and marches past Mateo sitting at the counter and out the door. The bell dings as it shuts behind her. Mateo gets up and follows her, casting one last confused look my way.

I don't fucking care.

I sit at the table by myself for a few minutes, watching the bubbles form and pop on the surface of my soda. *I don't care, I don't care.* The waitress comes by with a coffeepot in each hand.

"You okay, hon?" the waitress asks. "You look awful sad."

"I'm okay."

"Where'd your friends go?"

"They had to go home."

"Honey, I'll tell you something my mama told me a long time ago. Your girlfriends are the most important people you'll ever have in your life. You keep hold of them."

SIXTEEN
JUNE 30

"The night after I saw you at the Holler Up, I had a dream that we were swimming in that lake by my grandma's cabin in Emaleen," Bea says. "I started sinking, and you didn't see me. You kept swimming away; my mouth was full of water so I couldn't shout out to you. You swam away from me while I sank to the bottom." Bea scrubs at her eyes. "I'm so sorry, Camille. For driving away from you that day."

It's easy to think people forget about you when they walk away, like you never mattered at all, that you never shared a history. But of course that's not true. I'm still pissed at Bea, but it's not as if either of us has experience dealing with a problem like this.

I hug her. "I'll never let you sink, Bea. I promise. We'll always be friends." I step back, my hands on her shoulders. "Let's make a pact. Friends forever, no matter what?"

"Friends forever," she says. She smiles.

"Shall we spit swear on it? Just like in *My Girl*?"

"Ew, no!"

"Come on!" I hold my hand up to my mouth, pretending to spit into it.

Bang!

"Shit!" I jump, and a little *eeep* shoots out of Bea's mouth.

We swing around, trying to figure out where the noise is coming from.

"It's by the dumpsters," I say. "Nothing good comes from dumpsters."

Bea shakes her head vehemently.

Bang!

We stare at each other for a second, wide-eyed, and then grab hands and start running. "It's the hook guy!" Bea shrieks. "The hook guy."

"I think it's raccoons!"

"Raccoons with hooks!" Bea blurts out.

"That's bad, too!"

We keep running, zooming around the parking lot, hand in hand, back to the car.

Bea peeks into the front seat. "Shhh! Annabelle is still sleeping," she says, panting.

I look into the window. "I don't think I've ever seen anyone sleep that hard in my life." I doubt she'd wake up for anything, even psycho killers or ghost strippers.

Bea studies Annabelle, who is lying on her back, her mouth half-open, her legs propped over her steering wheel, her bare feet squished against the window. "How can she sleep like that?"

"We might as well let her sleep a little longer. Are you tired?"

Bea shakes her head. "Do you want to play Uno?"

I laugh. "You have Uno?"

She looks at me like I'm crazy. "I always have Uno, you know that." She gently opens the car's back door, takes a deck of Uno out of her bag, and holds it up.

We find an old picnic table on the side of the Boobie Bungalow under a parking light, and Bea deals out the cards. "This feels like the weirdest slumber party ever," she says.

"For sure." Over at the dumpster, the crashing noise continues.

"Will someone tell the neighbors to keep it down?" Bea says.

"Shut up!" I yell in the dumpster's direction.

Bang!

My Uno hand stinks, and Bea swiftly wins the round, as per usual. Bea is basically the undisputed Uno champion. She shuffles the deck and deals out another round, snapping each card down in a perfectly square pile.

"Remember when we thought our model horses came to life when we weren't there?" she says.

I laugh. "Yeah. God, we were so goofy back then."

"Why didn't you want to tell your parents?" Bea asks, arranging her cards in her hands. She asks me this so casually that I think for a moment that she's asked me something else.

"What a way to switch the subject—from model horses to telling my parents."

"You don't have to talk about it if you don't want to."

"No. I want to."

SEVENTEEN
JUNE 22

*H*ours later, after all my mom's friends are gone, and after my dad and brother, Chris, have come home, I go down to the kitchen. I open the fridge door and then close it again.

"What are you doing, Camille?" Mom asks.

"I'm just looking for something to eat."

"Please don't." She carries a big pot of water over to the sink and pours it into a colander. Water gushes out, followed by a tangle of spaghetti. "I'm making dinner."

Mom, I'm pregnant. I try the words out in my head and imagine her looking up at me with her glasses steamed over, her face filled with confusion, and then I'll have to say it again: *Mom, I'm pregnant.*

I can't do it.

My dad comes into the kitchen, but we don't say hi. He's

wearing his trucker's cap of invisibility, which is something he learned about from an agent at one of the writers' conferences he goes to. "Don't talk to me—I'm writing" is Sharpied across the orange brim. When he's wearing that, we aren't allowed to notice him. I watch while he opens the fridge, pours himself a glass of apple juice, and ghosts out of the kitchen and back to the closet he writes in. *Dad, I'm pregnant!* I think about shouting. I imagine him turning around, his eyes wide with shock.

I can't do it.

A big sob rises up and gets stuck in my throat. I turn around so my mom can't see my expression.

"Camille, can you set the table?" Mom says.

I open the utensil drawer and gather the silverware, trying to focus on what I'm doing. I bunch some spoons and forks in my hand and reach for a pile of napkins. I turn around and run straight into my mom. She's carrying a pot of pasta sauce; it slops out and splashes over both of us. The sauce is hot, and I jump back.

"Camille, watch what you're doing!"

"I'm sorry!" I burst into tears. "I'm sorry!"

"Sweetie, it's fine. Don't be so dramatic. It's only sauce. You didn't burn yourself, did you?" The sauce has splattered all over my mom's canvas apron, the one she's had since culinary school.

I shake my head.

She sets the pot down, grabs the washcloth, and dabs at the sauce stain on my shirt. We both smell like oregano and garlic. "It's nothing to cry over."

Chris wanders into the kitchen, eyes glued to his phone.

"When's dinner, Mother dearest?" he says. He looks up. "What happened? It looks like a murder scene in here."

Mom holds up her hand, the sign that means shut up. "Christopher, can you finish setting the table, please, while Camille changes?"

"On it." Chris puts his phone in his pocket and tiptoes through the sauce on the floor. He takes the silverware and napkins out of my hands. "Cheer up, buttercup," he says. "No sense crying over spilt spaghetti sauce."

I wipe my eyes with the backs of my hands and don't say anything.

I go upstairs and take my sauced-up shirt into the bathroom to soak. I look in the mirror as the sink fills. My eyes are bright red and swollen from crying, and there are tear tracks on my cheeks. I tie my hair back and splash water on my face. I look in the mirror again.

What are you going to do?

I'm going to tell them. I *have* to tell them, don't I? As soon as I get downstairs, as soon as I sit down at the table, I'm just going to say it.

Mom, Dad, I have something to tell you. I made a dumb mistake. I'm pregnant, and I don't know what to do.

I made a dumb mistake. I'm pregnant, and I don't know what to do.

I'll pretend I'm acting in a play. I'll pretend this isn't real life.

When I reach the second-to-the-last step, I go downstairs. I stop, frozen, unable to force my feet to keep going.

I hear a step squeak behind me. "Out of the way, face-ache,"

Chris says as he thumps past me. "Dinner waits for no man." Then he turns, an open geology textbook in his hands. "Why are you standing there anyway?"

I shake my head. "I don't know." I step onto the old shag pile carpet my dad says he'll replace with hardwood flooring, but never does. I follow Chris to the dining room where my parents are sitting, drinking their glasses of red wine and laughing about something.

Chris sits at the table in his usual spot, across from me. He starts reading his textbook.

I sit down. My palms are cold and sweating. How can palms be cold and sweating at the same time? I wipe them on my pants.

Mom and Dad, I have something to tell you. I made a dumb mistake. I'm pregnant, and I don't know what to do.

My dad dishes out the pasta and sets our plates in front of us. Alfredo sauce instead of my mom's homemade one.

"Put the book away, Christopher," my father says. "It's family time."

Chris holds his finger up, reads a little more, and then snaps the book shut and sets it by his plate. He looks at me. "What's going on with you today? You've got a face like a smacked ass."

"Christopher!" my mom says.

"Well, she does. Look at her."

Mom studies my face. "She looks perfectly normal."

"Just shut up, Christopher!" I hiss.

Chris pulls a look like I blasted him in the face. He holds his hands up. "Okay. Sorry. I surrender."

"Just . . . back off."

"Stop fighting, you two," Mom says, throwing us a look.

"Sorry." I stare down at my plate; the mass of noodles and white sauce looks disgusting.

"I thought we were having your homemade sauce, Beth," Dad says. "I'm not complaining; I love your Alfredo, too."

"It's not mine, I'm afraid." Mom points her fork at me. "We're having Paul Newman for dinner because Miss Clumsy over here ran straight into me and made me drop the pot."

"The things we love about you, kiddo." He winks at me.

Chris joins in on the fun. "All over the place, it looked like a bloodbath."

"It was an accident," I say. Mom does this all the time. First she says it's no big deal, and then she turns it into a funny story to tell other people, like I'm her source for jokes. I've overheard her telling people really personal things about me, especially her best friend, Karen, in one of their endless phone conversations—like how I jumped into the kiddie pool when I was three, fully dressed in a party dress; how at two I ate a cricket because my brother told me it was candy. How I am afraid of clowns and people blowing up balloons. How I scrape my teeth on my utensils when I eat. How I got my period and didn't tell her for months because I was too embarrassed.

I can hear my mom whispering the story to Karen, swearing her to secrecy, sighing. *You won't believe what Camille did.*

My dad won't tell anyone—in fact he won't mention it. Ever. He'll be beyond embarrassed. He'll try to push the image of me and a boy having sex out of his brain. But he won't be able to stop himself from thinking about it. He won't be able to look

117

at me, and we'll both have to live with it. For the rest of our lives.

I'll have done the stupidest thing of all—hooking up with a random guy I didn't really know and getting myself pregnant. No one will ever forget what I did. Ever.

"I'm sorry I bumped into you, Mom." My voice shakes. "I wasn't paying attention. I'm an idiot, okay? I got it." I drop my fork onto my plate and it clatters.

My dad, startled, looks to my mom for help.

"You aren't an idiot," Mom says.

"Yikes," Chris mutters, and then opens his textbook. "Drama."

Mom reaches over and puts her hand over mine. "It's okay. We're only kidding around with you."

"It's not funny. I don't like it." I pick up my fork. I try to take a bite of Alfredo. I try to swallow, but I can't force it down. The smell of Alfredo sauce hits me right in the face.

"Camille, are you okay?" Dad says.

I pull my hand from under my mom's and stand up. "I don't feel well." I bury my nose in my napkin and run upstairs to my bedroom.

It's dark and comforting under my grandma's old patchwork quilt. Its cheerful calico-print friendship squares and cherry-sprigged chain blocks always made me feel better. *Every little girl needs a security blanket*, my grandma had said when she handed it to me when I was six. The muslin back is worn smooth with multiple washings, but I can still make out the little label she sewed on the back: TO MY SWEET CAMILLE, WITH LOVE, GRANDMA.

I wonder what Grandma would think of me now. Her sweet Camille turned out to be not so sweet after all.

I hear a knock on my door. "Camille? It's Dad. Do you need anything? I have some Pepto in the fridge. Or how about some ginger ale?"

"I'm okay, Dad," I say, trying not to gag at the thought of Pepto-Bismol. "I just felt sick all of a sudden. I'm going to sleep."

My mom says something to him. I can make out the word *period*.

"Oh," Dad says. "That's all you, then, Beth."

My mom thinks I'm sick because I'm on my period. She thinks I have cramps. She would never imagine I'm sick because I'm pregnant.

I hear their footsteps fade as they walk away.

The waistband on my jeans feels too tight. The underwire on my bra presses hard against my rib cage. Am I already starting to get bigger? I wonder what my body will do next, and I'm scared of that. It's like my body is making decisions all on its own, and I can't do anything to make it stop. I want to go back in time and not do what I did. But I can't.

EIGHTEEN
JUNE 30

"I wish I could go back in time, too," Bea says. "I wouldn't abandon you like I did. It makes me feel awful that you didn't have anyone to talk to. I tell my mom everything, but I don't know if I could tell her I was pregnant, either."

"What's your reason?"

She folds her Uno hand. "I feel like I have to be perfect for them, never make them worry. You know, I've only texted with my mom a few times since we've been gone? Usually, we're, like, constantly texting."

"I can't imagine texting my mom that much. Our texts are strictly professional—where are you, what time are you coming home, take out the trash—that kind of thing. I don't know. Maybe I should text her more."

"I've never told you this before, but I always had this idea of my mom and me. I wanted us to be like the Gilmore Girls, constantly together, telling each other everything. Joking back and forth. I know that's silly now."

"I don't think that's silly. You're lucky to be close to your mom. I've always been jealous of that."

"What's going to happen when I go off to college, though? I can't keep calling my mom for stuff. It's like you said before. I can't expect my mom to wave a magic wand and make everything better."

"I'm sorry I said that," I say. "I was mad at you."

"But you were right. I guess another reason I got upset before was because you and Annabelle know so many things. You can make decisions for yourselves. I'm like a little kid compared to you two."

"Knowing things isn't that big of a deal. You can google stuff, like you did with the condoms. You're kind, Bea. Not many people are like that anymore."

Bea drops her cards and leans over the table, throwing her arms around me.

"Hey, you're messing up the discard pile," I say, although I hug her back.

Bea sits back, brushes at her eyes. She tidies the pile and gathers her cards. After a second she looks at me, her expression serious. "Do you think you'll ever tell them?"

"That all depends."

"On what?"

"On how I feel after this is all over." I play a wild card on top of Bea's yellow. "Blue," I say.

Bea wins again. And by then we're both exhausted. We head

back to the car and nudge Annabelle, but she swipes at us and goes back to sleep.

"Her disco nap is turning into a full-on sleep session," I say.

"Let's let her sleep until morning. Nothing will be open in Alamo anyway," Bea points out.

We get in the car. Bea gives me her pillow, bunches her sweatshirt under her head, and goes to sleep.

But I stay awake. The seat is too uncomfortable, and the darkness and the silence scare me.

I play Candy Crush on my phone on mute, but I can't concentrate on the game and I keep losing lives.

I wish I were home in my own bed. I wish this had never happened. But wishes are something you did when you were little when you blew out the candles on your cake, refusing to tell anyone because you knew the wish wouldn't come true if you did. You didn't know then how useless wishing was.

Maybe this is what being an adult is like—spending all your money on tires and gas and things like toilet paper and dish soap, and not depending on your parents to help you out. Having a budget to make sure you have enough money to get through the next shit storm. The thought of that depresses me. There has to be more to life than that.

My phone screen fades, the colorful candies shut off midcrush, my battery dead.

At least I'll have Bea with me when crap like that happens. And Annabelle, too. I'm not alone.

I finally fall asleep.

* * *

As soon as the sky begins to turn orange, I nudge Annabelle awake. "What's happening?"

"It's okay. Remember we had to stop in the night?"

"Oh, that," she says. "Sweet baby Jesus. I had the worst dream. I dreamed I slept in a car." She rubs her eyes and starts the car. Bea wakes up as soon as we start moving.

She bounces upright. "Back in business, ladies." One of the things I don't like about Bea is her morning cheerfulness.

I'm loaded on anxiety and adrenaline, which pretty much renders me unable to be cheerful or grumpy. I actually think I'm in some weird dimension, where I'm watching my life unfold from a window.

We pull out of the parking lot and stop at a doughnut shop a few exits away to use the bathroom, brush our teeth, and get breakfast. When Annabelle comes out of the bathroom stall, she's exchanged her Wendy Davis shirt for a plain black T-shirt. My braid got all messed up in the car, and I let it loose, not giving a crap that it's springing all over my head like Medusa's snakes. Bea changes into a sundress from her closet-on-the-go duffel bag, to which Annabelle gives the side-eye.

I'm craving sugar and grease like I never have in my life. I choose a chocolate cream doughnut coated in powdered sugar, a ham-and-cheese breakfast biscuit, and a large Sprite. Staying up all night makes me feel weird, like the world is tilting sideways and I'm sliding. Everything feels like a dream.

We eat our breakfast quickly, and I buy a dozen doughnuts and refill my Sprite.

I'm nearly there. I don't have far to go now.

The Rio Grande Valley has a harsh kind of beauty. We drive past wind farms, the windmills' huge white propellers slicing the sky. There are Mexican fruit stands everywhere. Big mesh bags of oranges and lemons are stacked in pyramids underneath ramshackle sheds. Billboards advertise in a mix of English and Spanish—a Dr Pepper sign says 23 SABORES BLENDED INTO ONE EXTRAORDINARY TASTE. INCONFUDIBLE! It's like the US and Mexico got together and decided to merge into one.

The closer we get to Alamo, the harder it is for me to stave off the nervousness. It starts to ramp up when we exit off the highway for Alamo.

In the town, the streets are lined with palm trees and all the shops have matching Spanish tile roofs. We pass RV parks and golf courses and signs for the wildlife sanctuary. At least half of the traffic on the road is United States border patrol cars.

"Where the heck is this place?" Annabelle says, scanning the street.

"There," Bea says. "I see a sign."

I bunch my hands, gripping them into tight fists.

"It will be okay," says Annabelle, her expression calm. "Try to breathe."

We leave the town center and follow each sign leading to the Hidalgo flea market. We can hear the music before we reach the parking lot. The market is inside an enormous corrugated steel structure, open on all sides.

"I want to run inside, grab those pills, and jump back in the car," I say.

"That's what we'll do, then," Bea says.

A man in an orange vest and a straw cowboy hat directs us to park Buzzi in a spot in the middle of a dusty field. We trudge our way through car-flattened grass and weeds. Annabelle kicks an old beer bottle all the way to the building, where she picks it up and tosses it into a steel oil drum.

Inside the market, people sit at picnic tables eating tamales. A man stands next to a tacos *al pastor* truck, slicing pieces from a huge cone of meat topped with a pineapple. He flicks a piece of pineapple off with his knife and catches it with a tortilla, handing it to the next person in a long line of customers. Other people leave a stand clutching cups filled with icy raspa. A Mexican band plays Tejano music while a bunch of people dance, scuffing their western boots against the dirt floor. A man with an accordion sings a Spanish song into a microphone. It's colorful and lively, and I wish I could enjoy it.

"This place is huge," Bea says. "It's going to take forever to find that pharmacy booth. Should we ask someone?"

I look down the line of booths selling cowboy boots and hats, jewelry, rugs, towels, furniture, cleaning supplies that line the inside of the building. It's crammed with people who jostle us as they walk past us. "Let's just go up and down the aisles."

After a few minutes of wandering, we find a *farmacia* tucked next to a flower cart and a booth selling pan dulce and churros.

A man wearing a cowboy hat, a plaid western shirt, and a bolo tie stands behind a table laid out with bottles and packages. We look through the table for the Cytotec, but all we find are boxes of cold medicine, Alka Seltzer, cough syrup, and aspirin. The man sees us looking and comes over.

"Can I help you find something?" he asks.

I clear my throat. "Cytotec? *Cytoteca?*"

"Don't have it." His eyes shift away from us. "Can't sell that anymore."

"It's for an ulcer?" I say.

He shrugs. "Like I said, I don't have it."

"Seriously, you don't have it?" Annabelle takes out a ten-dollar bill. "Can you look?" She holds out the money, and the man shifts his eyes from the money to Annabelle.

"Keep your money, *mija*. I don't have it. Last week the police raided a *farmacia* at the market in McAllen and took it all away. It's not worth going to jail, so I don't get it anymore."

"You'd go to jail?" I ask. Fear surges through me. "It is illegal?"

He shrugs again. His gaze shifts to a security guard standing near the doorway.

"Is there any other *farmacia* booth that sells it?" Annabelle asks.

"*No sé.*"

"Do you know any other place where we can buy it outside of the market?" I try again. "There must be somewhere. We've come a long way."

But he's done with us. A man in a denim shirt approaches and the booth owner shouts a greeting. He turns his back and starts in on a conversation in Spanish.

"Hey," Annabelle says. But the booth owner ignores us, talking away as though we're invisible.

"I knew it," I say. "Why would the police raid that other flea market if it isn't illegal?"

"It's probably illegal to sell the drug, not to have it, which is some bullshit."

"Maybe," I say, but I'm not convinced.

Bea doesn't add to the conversation. Her face is pale.

"Why don't you wait for us by the taco truck, Bea?" I say.

"No, I want to help." Her voice wavers, and I know she's scared.

We keep looking. Embarrassment and shame follow me down aisle after aisle. We find two other pharmacies, but no one sells Cytotec. One person acts like she doesn't know what we are talking about. She looks down at the floor and doesn't respond to any of our questions. I feel like every single person in the whole market knows exactly what we're up to—three dumb girls looking to get an over-the-counter abortion.

"So, it's Mexico," Annabelle says.

"Can we bring drugs across the border?" Bea whispers, darting a glance over her shoulder like a border patrol officer is listening in. "Maybe we'll get caught for smuggling drugs when we try to cross back into the US?"

I picture the border patrol putting us in handcuffs, hauling us off, and calling my parents to tell them I am in jail, that I tried to buy drugs in Mexico to abort my pregnancy. I swallow and shift from foot to foot. Suddenly I don't feel so good.

"Let's get something to drink, and we'll talk about it," Annabelle says.

Annabelle parks me at a picnic table and gets in line at the drink stand. She comes back with three large horchata drinks. "I don't see any option other than going to Mexico," she says. "We're, like, barely a mile to the border."

"Are you sure?" Bea asks. "It doesn't seem safe. I saw this thing on *Vice* about kidnapping and drug gangs there."

Annabelle shakes her head. "Americans cross the border all the time and come back okay, don't they?" But Annabelle says all this to the top of the picnic table. I don't think she's really any happier about going to Mexico than we are.

"What if we can't bring the pills back with us?" I say.

"You can take the first pills in Mexico," Annabelle says. "We can buy a bottle of aspirin and hide the rest of the Cytotec in the bottle. We'll buy some dumb souvenir and act like tourists."

I get out my phone. "There are three border crossings near us," I say. "It looks like Brownsville is the easiest one. We can cross into Mexico to Matamoros." I find a website with advice for traveling into Mexico. "If we leave Buzzi in a parking lot and walk in, we won't have to buy special insurance. The town is right there, so maybe we will find a *farmacia* close by."

Bea scrolls through her phone. "This website says to leave everything in the US apart from the money we need and to dress like we're poor so we won't be a target for kidnapping. To be honest, I don't even understand how we ended up here, searching for some illegal drug."

I close my eyes and try to remain calm. "The reason we're

here, Bea," I say—and let's be real, no one is buying the calm act—"is because a man following a law most certainly made up by another man—"

"Most *definitely*," Annabelle throws in.

"—decided that I, a seventeen-year-old girl in the top ten percent of her class—"

"That's a slight exaggeration," Bea says.

"Whatever, he decided that I shouldn't have the right to make choices about my own body. He prevented me from having an abortion at a real clinic. He ruled against me, Bea. He made the decision *for* me."

"Tell her about the judge, Camille."

NINETEEN

JUNE 27

"Camille Winchester." Mr. Daniels sorts through the stack of papers on his desk. "This is about a judicial bypass for an abortion?"

I nod. My face burns red with embarrassment that Mr. Daniels knows I'm pregnant. That he knows something about me that I don't want anyone to know.

"Have a seat, and let's get acquainted." He waves to a folding chair and I sit. He pushes away from his desk with both hands and wheels his desk chair over to me by paddling his feet on the floor. He stops in front of my chair and leans forward, dangling his wrists over his knees. A Mickey Mouse watch adorns his left wrist. "Now, I understand you're looking to get an abortion, and you don't want to let Mom and Dad know, is that right?"

I'm a little skeeved out by him calling my parents "Mom and

Dad," as if they are his parents, too. I nod and stare at my shoes. There's a big scuff mark across one toe, and I hide the shoe behind my ankle. I should have worn the new ballet flats my mom bought on sale for school that are tucked away on the top shelf of my closet.

"Can you tell me why you can't tell Mom and Dad? Are you afraid of them?"

I jerk my head up. "No!"

"Well, then, why won't you tell them?" A whiff of aftershave drifts my way.

The clock hanging over his desk is a Mickey Mouse one. Mickey's gloved hands are the clock's hands, and his eyes swing back and forth as the clock ticks.

"You're going to have to help me, Miss Winchester, otherwise I can't advise Judge on what is best for you." He's talking to me in that way adults sometimes talk to small children: that fake friendliness that even little kids don't believe.

"I just don't want to tell them, and that's really it, I guess."

"Is it a spiritual reason? Are we a religious household?" He foot-wheels over to his desk, picks up a pen and pad of paper, and shoves off the desk to sail back to me, his legs stretched out. He clicks on the pen and holds it up, waiting for my response.

"No. We aren't." My hands are shaking and I tuck them under my legs.

He lowers the pen. Unclicks it.

"It's nothing like that, I mean. I don't want to disappoint them. I'd rather just do this . . . and pretend it never happened."

"I don't think it's in your best interest to pretend your

pregnancy didn't happen. We don't want an unplanned pregnancy to happen again, do we?"

He writes something down and then bounces the pen on the notebook, unclicking it. "Now, Miss Winchester. In my opinion, I think you should tell Mom and Dad, but you can present your case to the judge because that is your right to do so."

He holds out his hand, and I shake it. His palm is cold. "I'll see you in Judge's chambers."

I close the door behind me, and I can hear him shuffling that dumb chair around. Part of me wants to run away from all of this and hide, and another part of me wants to go back into that office, yank the Mickey Mouse clock off the wall, and stomp it to pieces with my scuffed-up shoes.

The real me goes into the ladies' room and pukes.

I walk across the street to the courtyard in front of the courthouse to meet Nicole, the lawyer who Jane's Due Process, the abortion rights nonprofit, hired for me. She's wearing a gray pencil skirt and jacket and has short blond hair. Just like when I met her yesterday, she's kind and friendly.

"How did your first appointment at Planned Parenthood go yesterday?"

I shrug. "Okay, I guess. A little embarrassing."

"I'm glad you got in so quickly; sometimes it can take a week or two. You have all your documentation and proof of the appointment? The judge will want to see that."

I hold up the folder.

"Did you book your second appointment?"

I nod. "Yes, for a week from Monday." I cross my fingers when

I say this because if I don't get the bypass, I'll have to tell my parents I'm pregnant, and then ask them to sign this awful consent form which is six pages long and has to be notarized. It includes sentences like *I understand the abortion will result in the death of the fetus.* It lists a ton of unlikely things that can happen to me with an abortion, including hemorrhaging, blood clots, a possible hysterectomy, a hole in the uterus, and sterility, even though my Planned Parenthood doctor told me that abortion is safer than a colonoscopy or having a penicillin shot. I got so mad when I read all that. How can the state of Texas lie to women so blatantly?

"I know you're prepared for this, Camille," Nicole says as we walk upstairs to the judge's chamber. "The judge can't help but see that you are mature enough to handle making this decision on your own."

I start to get nervous, way nervous. I don't think I can sit in a roomful of men and answer personal questions about myself. Nicole said he might ask me questions about that pamphlet Planned Parenthood gave me about abortion, which I barely had time to read. I'll pretend to be someone else, a character from a play. I flip through all the roles I've played over the years. But I can't think of any character who would work. Not Blanche from *Streetcar.* Not Ophelia or Juliet and for sure not Desdemona, who Othello smothered to death. I can't think of any female character who could or would rise to this occasion. And that makes me more upset. I've never noticed how weak these characters are. How they've never had a say in their own lives.

"You okay?" Nicole asks.

"Who will be in there? I mean, why are there so many people?"

"Well, the judge, the court reporter—in case we need a transcript to file an appeal—and the guardian ad litem, whom you already know."

I picture that guy rolling into the judge's room in that chair of his, all decked out in his Mickey Mouse best. "I'm not sure about Mr. Daniels," I say. "I don't think he liked me very much. He told me straight off that I should tell my parents."

Nicole pauses on a stair step. She sighs. "I don't know about some of these people the judge assigns. I had a priest last week—a Catholic priest of all people. Of course he fought for the girl to go through with her pregnancy."

"What if that happens to me?" I ask.

Nicole takes me into a little hallway in front of the restrooms. "It's okay, Camille. I'm here with you." She takes me by the shoulders. "Look at me. Try to calm down. I know this is daunting, but I'm with you. You don't have to do this alone."

I try to breathe like Nicole says. But every time I get control of myself, I think about having to cancel that appointment, and I start to choke up again.

"I'm not going to lie; it can be very daunting to discuss your personal life with a bunch of strangers, especially ones you're trying to convince," Nicole says. "But I'll be with you. I'll be there to support you."

After a couple of minutes, the ball of tears starts to back down. But I know it's there, right at the surface.

"I want you to tell yourself that this is your right. You deserve to be heard, okay?"

"Okay."

Nicole looks at her watch. "We have to go in now."

We enter the main hall, and a uniformed police officer opens the door to the judge's chamber. A black-robed judge sits behind a desk, and he barely looks up when we enter the room. He's around seventy or so, and a horseshoe of hair surrounds a bald spot. A bowl of foil-wrapped candy sits on his desk. A woman in a pink sweater set and a green plaid skirt sits behind a small keyboard, waiting, her hands in her lap. Her long blond hair is clipped back on each side with mismatched barrettes—one tortoiseshell, one brown. And then there is Mr. Daniels. He smiles when he sees me, but I just nod.

It smells like old library books and dusty curtains, and I swallow back the nausea. I swear to God, if I puke in here . . .

Nicole and I sit on chairs in front of the judge. I put my purse on the floor neatly and tuck my scuffed shoes under the chair. I force myself to sit up straight and hold my head high. *This is my right. I deserve to be heard. This is my right. I deserve to be heard.*

Nicole presents my case, explaining that I wish a judicial bypass to get an abortion. The judge listens, his hands on top of a manila folder with my name on it. After Nicole finishes, the judge opens the folder, squints at the paper on top, and then closes it. "Now, Miss Winchester, tell me a bit about yourself. Where you live, where you work, where you go to school."

I stumble through all the answers, trying to keep eye contact with the judge like Nicole said. But it feels too personal, so I focus on the bridge of his nose instead. The judge smiles when I tell him I'm an actor.

"I'm a theater buff myself," he says. "Been in some community plays, *The Music Man*, *Carousel*. Have you been in any of those?"

I loathe both of those musicals with a personal hellish passion. There isn't a decent female role in either one. The best you can hope for is dopey Marian the Librarian in *The Music Man*, who falls in love with a man she knows is a con man, or *Carousel*'s stupid Louise, who says her father's ghost slap felt like a kiss.

I sit up tall and smile. *This is my right. I deserve to be heard.* "I haven't. I'm not in many musicals. I mean, the theater group I belong to is mostly Shakespearean, and we focus on other classic playwrights like Chekhov, Hellman, Ibsen. I've done some high school musicals, like Sondheim ones, but I'm not much of a singer."

And then he does something that wipes that phony smile off my face. He starts to sing a song from *Carousel*. His voice is deep, and he sounds like an old-fashioned crooner, like he could sing in a barbershop quartet.

I want to slap my hands over my ears.

"Walk on, walk on, with hope in your heart! And you'll never walk alone!" He points a finger at me.

The court reporter keeps typing, and somehow it makes me feel better that his stupid performance is being copied into the permanent court report.

Finally the judge stops singing. The room is silent. Nicole's cell phone vibrates; she glances at the number and then slips the phone into her pocket.

"I think the words to that tune are incredibly inspiring and uplifting," the judge says.

"Okay," is all I say.

"You have a job, Miss Winchester?"

"I work at an ice cream stand called Iggy's."

"Save up your money, or do you spend it quick?"

I clear my throat. "I save. For school, I mean. For college. I want to study acting?" I don't know why I say this like it's a question.

"You don't care for shopping or makeup?"

"I'm saving all my money for school."

"Drama school is probably expensive."

"Yes."

He sits back in his chair and studies me. "The chance of making a successful career in acting is pretty slim, did you know that?"

"Yes."

He shakes his head and frowns. "So many kids these days are choosing to study things like art or drama or humanities that won't land a ding-dang job. All they end up with is crushing debt that follows them around for years."

"I'm going to minor in accounting." Those words slip out of my mouth. I'm horrible at math. No way would I study accounting. I feel like I've entered an improv class, "yes, and"-ing the judge.

He nods. "That's a very good choice. Accounting will help you manage your budget when you get married and have a family of your own."

"That's a good point," I say, nodding. "I really love numbers.

They are so . . . so useful in many walks of life." I can't believe the crap I'm saying.

"And how did you get pregnant?" His switch in subjects startles me. He opens the folder and scans it as though the story of the conception might be listed there. "Were you raped?"

"No!" The word comes out sharper than I mean it to. I clear my throat. "No, I mean. Would that matter?"

He closes the folder and sets his hands on top of it, linking his fingers together. "Do you love that fella of yours?"

"He's not my fella anymore. Fellow. I . . . I mean, no, I don't love him." I forgot about telling the judge what he wants to hear. I forgot to "yes, and" him.

The judge raises his eyebrows. "You had intercourse with him anyway? That doesn't show good judgment, wouldn't you agree?"

"I don't know." I'm doing a terrible job. I'm only digging myself in deeper. I really don't like the way he said *intercourse*. I wish Mr. Daniels didn't look so interested in my personal life. I'm starting to think the both of them are only trying to humiliate me.

This is my right. I deserve to be heard.

"Does this fella know about your pregnancy?"

I shake my head.

"Say yes or no," the judge says. "The court reporter needs a verbal response."

"No," I say, directing my answer toward the court reporter and not him.

"Have you thought of all your options? No need to rush into something as terrible as abortion when you can find a better solution such as adoption."

"I don't want the other solution," I say, looking the judge right in the eye. "I know all the facts; I read that booklet, and I'm not continuing this pregnancy." My voice is high and thin. "I've already had the required counseling and ultrasound. I'm following the rules. I've made up my mind."

"What do you think, Tony?" The judge addresses Mr. Daniels.

"It's in my professional opinion that she inform Mom and Dad. She comes from a loving home, and I believe not telling them could cause a problem in the family later on down the road. At this point I feel she's simply embarrassed and doesn't want to admit what she's done."

What I've done. I want to stand up and yell at these old men and tell them a boy had something to do with it, too.

"I see no reason for the court to intervene," Mr. Daniels says.

"Miss Winchester," the judge says. "I sang 'You'll Never Walk Alone' because I think it applies to your situation. Sometimes in life, we aren't dealt the hand that we want. Sometimes the good Lord puts a challenge in our way to make us better people. And for you that challenge is motherhood."

Nicole does the best she can to change the judge's mind, but it's clear he'd already decided before we walked in here. I hadn't done a good enough job getting Mr. Daniels on my side. I should have told him I was afraid of my dad. But the thought of saying such an awful lie turns me cold.

We go out into the hall to wait for the decision. Nicole squeezes my shoulder. "Try to relax," she says. "It shouldn't be too long."

"I hate those men," I say. "I want to punch them in the face."

I don't know where to stand. I don't know what to do with my hands. Across from me, the courtroom doors open and people pour out. I don't want anyone to look at me. If I feel someone's eyes land on me, I swear I'll lose it.

There's a deep feeling of dread building inside me, and I know the judge is not going to give his permission. I did a stupid thing, and he won't let me get away with it.

"I don't think I did a good job," I say.

"You did a great job, Camille. You were confident; you spoke well."

"I don't think so."

The judge's door opens and the bailiff steps out. He waves us back inside. The judge sits behind his desk. Mr. Daniels stands beside him. The judge doesn't ask us to sit.

"Miss Winchester," he says. "I can't in good conscience as a father and a Christian give you the bypass. I know you want to terminate your pregnancy, and that is your right to do so. However, I don't think you've proved yourself mature enough to make this decision on your own."

He thinks I am a child, a dumbass kid who is deluded enough to think she can make a living as an actor; who makes stupid mistakes like getting knocked up by a guy she doesn't love. I make immature decisions, one after the other, just like my parents always say. The judge doesn't even know me and yet he saw it right away.

"Your parents sound like good people, and I believe they should be involved in this important decision. I think you'll thank me for it in the end."

The bailiff ushers us to the door.

Nicole and I stand outside.

"That's certainly not the outcome I had hoped for," Nicole says. "We can appeal, Camille. I know this is disappointing, but appeals happen all the time. The court has to rehear the case five days after we appeal, which takes us at least a week. Trouble is, we're bumping up against the Fourth of July, so it'll be a little longer. At least a couple of weeks. And to be honest, an appeal is rarely granted."

"I guess I'll have to tell my parents after all." But the thought of telling them knocks the wind out of me. "Get their permission." I can't breathe.

Nicole smiles. "What was up with that singing?"

"Awkward." I try to smile, but my chin starts to tremble.

"You going to be okay?" she asks.

I nod. My eyes are swimming with tears I don't want her to see. "I have to go to the bathroom," I say.

She pats me on the arm. "Call Jane's Due Process if you need us, okay?"

I'm halfway down the hall when I hear a shout. "Miss!" The court reporter is trotting toward me, her heels tapping on the floor, her hand outstretched. "Miss Winchester," she says. "You dropped this." She catches up to me and hands me a folded paper.

"Oh, I'm sorry." I take the paper, but I don't recognize it. "I don't think this is mine," I say, handing it back to her. "Maybe someone else dropped it."

She steps back and shakes her head, and I notice that there is a hole in her pink sweater set, right by the elbow, and little balls of wool have accumulated along the inside of her sleeves. And up close her makeup is smudged under her eyes. "Take it." She reaches out for my hand and folds my fingers around it. Her hands are warm and damp, and she doesn't let go. "Take it."

The bailiff pokes his head out of the judge's room and calls to her. She doesn't say anything else. I see her wipe her eyes with the palms of her hands as she walks back. And then she pulls the edge of her cardigan down and enters the room.

I open the paper. On it are scribbled the words:

Self-abortion possible through a medication called Cytotec or Cytoteca. Available at flea markets near the border or in Mexico. Hidalgo flea market in Alamo, Texas, usually has it. Ask for Cytotec or Cytoteca, and say you have an ulcer. $13 a pill. Buy at least a dozen pills, and go to womenonweb.org for instructions. PS Important to use within twelve weeks. DO NOT USE AFTER TWELVE WEEKS.

TWENTY
JULY 1

"Such a fucking creep, right? I can't believe he sang," Annabelle says. "And that dumb guy with the Mickey Mouse stuff. There oughtta be a law about grown men wearing children's cartoon stuff."

"Right?" I say. "It's like he's wearing that stuff to relate to kids or something."

"No one's buying it, dude," Annabelle says. "That court reporter is a shero, though."

"I wonder how many girls she's given that note to," I say. "I kind of feel like I should tell her that no one at the flea market carries Cytotec anymore. I mean, she could lose her job."

Bea doesn't say anything. She's scrolling through her phone. "You don't know that for sure," she says. She looks up from her phone. "You don't know that lady from Adam, Camille."

"We won't stay long. We'll be all right," I tell her.

"I still say—"

"You don't have to go!" Annabelle glares at her. "You can stay on the border, how about that?"

Bea presses her mouth, like she's physically holding her words in. She looks over at the dancers. A little girl holds her frilly skirt in one hand and swishes it back and forth to the music. Another man holds his little girl and dances with her, smiling.

"You've been to Mexico before," I say. "Why are you so scared now?"

"Yeah, Cancún and Puerto Vallarta! The border towns are different. Even the State Department website says so." She holds her phone up. I catch a glimpse of the American flag on the screen before she puts it down.

"I know you're worried, Bea," I say. "But I have to do this."

"We're too close," Annabelle says. She's fuming. "Besides, it's Camille's choice to have an abortion, not yours. I told you that on the phone."

A man next to us at the table lifts his head from his tacos when he hears her say *abortion*. A few people stare at us.

"What? Does that bother you? Abortion! Abortion! Abortion!" Annabelle says, looking pointedly at him. "Not exactly something you would know about since you don't have a uterus."

"Okay, I think we're done." I stand up and toss my cup into the garbage can. "Jeez, Annabelle."

"Sorry," she says, not looking sorry at all.

Bea shakes her head, mutters something under her breath, and stands up.

"Where are you going?" Annabelle asks.

"I'm going to get more horchata," she snaps.

"Wait a second. I'll go with you."

"Suit yourself," Bea mumbles.

"Chica!" Over at a nearby picnic table, an old woman with two little girls in braids and matching *Frozen* T-shirts waves to me. She says something in Spanish, and I start to walk away because I think she's going to shout at me about Annabelle, but she calls me again.

The older of the little girls rushes over. "My *abuela* says not to go to Matamoros. She says there are bad men there."

"We're only going for a little while. Maybe an hour."

The girl translates to her grandma, who clasps her hands together and waves them, a pleading look on her face.

"Abuela says don't go. She says to go to Nuevo Progreso. We go there all the time. It's not very far away."

The girl's grandmother says something else and the girl smiles. "Abuela says she hopes that you listen to her."

The woman's kindness reminds me of my own grandma. She used to take me to farmers' markets and stuff before she moved into the nursing home. My grandma would have bought me a *Frozen* T-shirt to wear, too. "Tell your grandma that we won't go to Matamoros. I promise."

The little girl tells her grandma what I said, and she smiles.

Bea and Annabelle come back with three horchatas, and we leave the market.

We pull out onto the highway and follow the directions on Google Maps. It's not very far, about a half hour away.

"So, we're going to Mexico," Annabelle says. "Just like in that movie *Thelma & Louise*."

"I don't think they ever got to Mexico," I say. "Didn't they drive over a cliff before that happened?"

"Oh god, don't! Don't say that's the next thing coming our way." Annabelle starts to laugh.

"Now, you get a grip, Louise," I say, quoting the movie. "Just drive us to goddamn Mexico."

Annabelle speeds up. "I'm drivin'."

"I never saw that movie," Bea says to herself, but Annabelle hears her.

"You should see it, Bea," Annabelle says. "It's a classic."

"Is it rated *R*?"

"I think so."

"I don't need to see it."

Annabelle studies Bea in the rearview mirror for a moment and then returns her attention to the road.

"You know that part in *Thelma & Louise*?" I ask Annabelle. "Where Thelma asks Louise what's the one thing that scares her the most?"

Annabelle thinks for a moment. "Oh, and she says getting old and living with a little dog by herself?"

"Yeah. I used to be afraid of not getting the part I wanted at the Globe, but that's not exactly a long-term fear. But now, I have so many fears I can't settle on the one thing that scares me the most. Right now, it's this big-ass mistake I made. I've lost so much already. How many friends and opportunities did I miss at Willow? And then there's Léo. Maybe something good would have come out of that." Sadness sinks over me, thinking of being with Léo on that bank, and how that will never happen again. "What's your biggest fear?"

Annabelle doesn't say anything for a long while. And then she speaks: "I'm afraid of letting people down."

I'm surprised by her answer. "You could never let anyone down, Annabelle. Look how you've helped me. Look how hard you worked to get to RADA and how proud you've made Mr. Knight and Tracy. They're already getting international students because of you. You're, like, his best advertisement."

"I don't think that's true." She puts on her turn signal and gets into the next lane.

"Well, I think so, even if you don't," I say.

"If you say so," she says.

"I do say so."

I watch her for a long while, waiting for her to say more, but she doesn't.

TWENTY-ONE

*W*e exit off the highway to Progreso, on the US side of the border, and after a couple of stoplights we follow the sign to the international bridge. Palm tree after palm tree lines the streets of the town. Annabelle parks the car in the border crossing lot, and we climb out. I pull the seat forward, but Bea doesn't get out of the back seat.

"I'm not going," Bea says, staring straight ahead, her jaw set. "It's too dangerous."

"All right." Annabelle hands her the keys. "Have it your way."

"It's okay, Bea," I say. "I don't want you to do anything you don't want to do."

"But for God's sakes, don't sit in the car," Annabelle says. "You'll bake."

"Whatever." Bea climbs out and heads to a nearby ice cream stand. She sits under a patio umbrella, facing away from us.

I'm about to call to her when Annabelle cuts me off.

"Forget it," Annabelle says. "It's her decision. Let's go."

We follow a group of people through a turnstile and past an adobe building. Next to the building is a little garden with giant terra cotta chickens. For some reason, the chickens make me feel calmer. It's like nothing bad can happen to you when giant chicken statues are part of the situation.

"Don't be mad at Bea, Annabelle," I say. "She's trying her hardest to be a good friend. But what I'm doing goes against everything she believes."

"I don't care what she believes," Annabelle says, "just as long as she keeps those thoughts to herself."

We enter a covered walkway that spans the bridge. Green fields stretch ahead of us, and the Rio Grande flows beneath us. I always thought it would be a gushing waterway, but it barely qualifies as a river. A scraggly line of trees and bushes border each side of the water, and it looks more like a creek, something you could swim across in about twenty strokes. My creek at the Globe is wider than this one.

In the middle of the bridge, there's a red line that divides the American and Mexican borders. We step over the line and into Mexico. It feels weird to enter another country like that. People are straddling the line and taking selfies. I could take a selfie on that line, smiling away like I'm having the best time of my life: *Half in and half out! #Mexico #America #yolo*

People would be jealous of me and my *fun in the Mexico sun!* They wouldn't have to know the real picture should be me standing in front of a pharmacy: *Looking for Cytoteca to end a pregnancy! #abortion #ashamed*

We reach the end of the bridge. Two boys shove baseball caps through the fence and wave them, begging us for money. Annabelle pretends not to notice and keeps walking, but I can't help looking through the slats at them. One is little, maybe six or seven. The other looks a bit older but not by much. I dig into my purse and drop a dollar into each hat. The boys jerk the hats back through the fence and scoop out the money. I run to catch up with Annabelle, my flip-flops smacking the concrete.

After a few minutes we see a sign over a cement building that reads BIENVENIDO A MEXICO. A long line of cars wait at the crossing, but we follow the other pedestrians into a building where a border crossing guard stops us and asks us our business in Mexico. We tell them we're going to shop and have a look around for the day. We pass through another turnstile that dumps us onto the streets of Nuevo Progreso.

It's like a different world. Traffic clogs the dusty streets and people blare their horns. Some of the sidewalks are busted up, and the buildings are janky, with peeling paint on plywood billboards out front. But everything is so colorful, and the shopkeepers shouting out to people are cheerful. On the sidewalks, people sit in lawn chairs next to open suitcases lined with silver jewelry and boxes of knock-off designer handbags. Men hold out flyers advertising all-you-can-drink bars written in English and Spanish. We walk past line after line of painted terra cotta pots and clay chimineas. Tejano music pours out of the shops. Street food stands are everywhere, and the smell of tortillas cooking makes me hungry again. It feels like a never-ending carnival.

Several men holding beer bottles catcall us as we walk by. "Don't say anything!" I say to Annabelle.

"Don't worry," she whispers, linking her arm through mine.

About a block ahead, next to a health clinic, there's a sign that says AZTECA FARMACIA. The shop looks like any other pharmacy I've ever been in. There are several people, Mexican and American, waiting in line. The Americans look nervous. I hear an older man ask for Viagra while his much younger wife shifts from foot to foot next to him, her cheeks pink with embarrassment.

I get in line behind them. My heart is roaring in my ears, and I try to breathe in and out to calm down, like I do before I go onstage. But it isn't working. What if the same thing happens like it did when I tried to buy the pregnancy test? What if the pharmacist makes me explain why I want the Cytotec? What if everyone in the shop overhears?

"I can't do this, Annabelle," I whisper. "I'm sure he won't let us have it. Let's just go."

"If that old dude can get Viagra, I'm sure we can get the Cytotec."

I shake my head and back toward the door.

"We've come this far! We can't back out now. Look, I'll go up and ask," she says. "Hang out there and don't worry." She points to a rack selling Mexican candies. She picks up a bottle of aspirin and gets in line.

I stand by the racks and stare at the unfamiliar candy, the

little pucks of De La Rosa Mazapan, the plastic bags of Pica Fresa and Bubbaloo. Two little boys in blue jeans and T-shirts push each other for their chance to turn the rack. They grab packs and shake and squeeze each one before shoving it back into its slot and grabbing another. I remember doing that when I was a kid, spending my birthday money on candy, walking up and down the grocery store aisle while my mother shopped, weighing the merits of Starbursts versus Nerds and Kit Kats versus Twix, like it was the most important decision I had to make. And maybe it was.

The memory of that, the cheerful packs of candy on the rack, the hopefulness of the boys sends a wave of sadness through me that feels like the worst homesickness I've ever felt. I'm going to cry. I'm going to burst into tears, and everyone is going to turn and stare at the hysterical American throwing a fit in the pharmacy.

I step away from the rack and wait by the door, wanting to be anywhere but here.

Annabelle's turn comes. I try not to stare at her in case the pharmacist notices me freaking out and gets suspicious. My palms start to sweat. This is worse than the time I had stage fright during a production of *The Winter's Tale* so bad that Mr. Knight had to physically push me onto the stage.

Annabelle asks the pharmacist for the Cytotec.

He pulls a box off the shelf, and Annabelle hands over the money. The pharmacist slips the box and the bottles into a paper bag and moves on to the next customer.

We hurry out of the shop, and Annabelle exhales and hands me the bag. Her hands are shaking, too. We step into a little alley between the pharmacy and a market called Oxxo.

I take out the box and slide out one of the packs. Each pill is packaged in its own little compartment. I should be happy that I finally have the pills. I'm terrified.

"How many do you start with again?"

"Four." I try to take the pills out of the packet, but my hands are trembling too hard to get the foil off the back.

"Here." Annabelle takes the pack, pops out four, and dumps them in my palm. I put each one under my tongue. They taste so bitter, I have to resist the urge to spit them out.

"How long do we wait?" she asks.

I'm too scared to open my mouth to speak in case the pills come out from under my tongue, so I hold my fingers up in a three and a zero.

Annabelle shoves the box in her tote bag and sets the timer on her phone for thirty minutes. And we wait, standing in the alley, leaning against a chipped adobe wall, not speaking.

Thirty minutes feels like forever when you're standing in a hot alley with abortion pills under your tongue. Annabelle must feel the same way because she keeps looking at the timer. My mouth is dry, and the pills don't seem to be dissolving like they should.

Two police officers come up the alley from the other direction, automatic weapons slung over their shoulders.

"Shit," Annabelle whispers.

I suck in my breath. The policemen look menacing with those guns. I imagine them pointing them at us. I imagine them searching us, finding the pills, and hauling us off to jail.

"They've seen us," she mumbles. "Smile when they come up. Acting skills at the ready."

My heart speeds up. I nearly swallow the pills from fear.

The policemen pass us. They don't look at us. They are laughing at something, acting normal, like normal people.

I let out my breath, and Annabelle closes her eyes.

Annabelle's phone alarm goes off. I spit what's left of the pills out in my hand, like the instructions say. But they don't look much different from when I put them in.

"Should I put these back in for a little while longer?" I ask.

Annabelle studies the pills in my hand. "Maybe the medicine is on the outside, like in a thin coating?"

"Maybe."

"I suppose it wouldn't hurt to put them back in again?" She sets the alarm. "Let's do another fifteen minutes."

"These are so gross," I say. I put them back in my mouth and I wait. Fifteen minutes later, I spit them out in my hand. They've dissolved into tiny chips.

Annabelle empties the aspirin bottle into a nearby trash can and pops each Cytotec pill out of the pack and drops them into the aspirin bottle. She rubs the bottle against the building to make it look old, like I've been carrying it in my purse forever. I'm impressed that she knew to do that.

I hide the bottle inside my makeup bag between my blush and mascara. We buy a sombrero and a piñata at a booth, head to the crossing. As we step over the line, taking us back to the United States, my phone dings with a message from Bea.

I hope you're okay. I wish I would have come now. Love you . . .

TWENTY-TWO

"Don't touch that remote," Bea says. I've just finished taking a shower at the dingy motel back in Alamo. "You don't know what's come across it. I watched this thing on *Danger Land* where they took swabs of hotel remotes, and you wouldn't believe what they found. And I took the bedspreads off because they never wash them."

"Duly noted," I say, lying down. "Where's Annabelle?" She hasn't said a word to Bea since we've been back. I think she's still mad at her for ditching us at the border. I hate being in the middle like this, but I'm not going to try to fix it, either; that's up to Annabelle and Bea.

"Picking up dinner."

The beds are hard and the pillows flat. I stack two under my head and take out my phone. I need to text my mom, but I don't know what to tell her. I put it down, and then I pick it up again.

Hey, just checking in, I type. *Having fun, learning lots. Willow is amazing.*

Mom immediately responds. *Great. You have a good time. Daddy and I miss you. I don't know about Chris, though! I think he's already hoping to have your room for some sort of virtual reality video thing when you go off to college.*

Annabelle comes in holding a pizza box in one hand and a bag with salads in it in the other.

That's a big surprise. Gotta go! Dinner's here.

Enjoy. Love you, honey.

We sit around the little table and pass around the salad. "It sucks that I can't tell my mom," I say.

"It's hard to talk to parents about stuff like this," Annabelle says.

"I tell my mom everything," Bea says.

"Yeah, well, that's because you've never done anything like this," I point out. "I mean, what have you ever done to make your parents mad? I can't think of anything."

Bea takes a bite of her pizza and chews. "How about that time I signed up for twenty angels off the church Christmas tree? I didn't think it would be that expensive to buy toys for twenty kids, but it was. My mom had to pay for them."

Annabelle stares at Bea, her slice of pizza halfway to her mouth. "Seriously? That's the worst thing you've done? You volunteered to buy too many Christmas presents for children in need?"

"Yeah," Bea says, raising her eyebrows. "It was bad. My mom was really mad about it."

Annabelle puts her pizza down and wipes the grease off her fingers. "Wow," she says. "Just . . . wow."

Bea shrugs. "You wouldn't say that if you'd been there."

"What about you, Annabelle?" I ask.

She leans her elbow on the table and cups her chin in her hand. "Well, let's see. My parents weren't too happy with me being a Planned Parenthood clinic volunteer. My dad wouldn't talk to me for days after I told him. He's a huge Republican, just loves, loves Rick Perry. Isn't all that fond of President Obama, that's for sure. Plus he hates how open people are about sex now. He says Planned Parenthood encourages people to have sex. Or *relations*, as he calls it."

"My parents would kill me if I even thought about having *relations*," Bea says. "We don't talk about that kind of stuff at my house. I don't think I've ever even said the V-word at home."

"The V-word?" Annabelle directs a long look at Bea.

"You know."

"Do you mean *vagina*?"

"Yeah, that."

I press my mouth shut hard so I don't burst out laughing.

"You can't say it, can you?" Annabelle continues.

"Yes, I can!" Bea says. She picks up another slice of pizza and crams it in her mouth.

"So, say it."

Bea takes forever to chew and swallow. "Um . . . vagina," she whispers.

Annabelle puts her hand behind her ear. "What?"

"Vagina!" Bea raises her voice. "There, I said it. I told you I could."

Annabelle picks up her slice again. "In England they made us yell all sorts of swear words onstage, one by one. It's supposed to break through our inhibitions, they told us. We had to read them off a list. Really filthy words, too. Did you know *fanny* means vagina in England?"

"I'm not sure I could say *vagina* onstage. Definitely not the C-word," I say. "It seems too, I don't know . . . embarrassing."

"That's the point," Annabelle says. "To break through all of that. Besides, people should be able to call a vagina a vagina, for fuck's sake. Why be embarrassed about it? I mean, did you get pregnant through an immaculate conception?" she asks, teasing.

"No."

"You can have sex with boys, so you should be able to talk about your vagina."

"Well, then, that lets me off the hook because I won't have sex until I get married," Bea says.

"She made a vow of purity in her church," I say.

"Really?" Annabelle asks.

"Show her your ring, Bea."

Bea wiggles her ring off her finger and hands it to Annabelle.

Annabelle holds the ring between her thumb and forefinger. *"I will wait for my beloved,"* she says, reading the inscription on the front of the ring. "Did your parents make you do this or did the church?"

"No one made me. The church won't let us take the vow if it

isn't our choice. We have to come to the idea on our own, but our parents present the rings."

"Her church had a father-daughter purity ball," I say. "Bea wore this beautiful white ball gown, and her dad wore a tuxedo."

"Our dads were our dates," Bea says. "There was a big cake and everything."

"Gotta love cake." Annabelle hands her the ring back. "Is your boyfriend religious, too?"

"Mateo? No. His parents are Catholic, but he's not interested, so they don't force him to go or anything. I think he goes to Mass on Christmas, but that's about it." She holds her hand up, studying the ring like she's seeing it for the first time. "Sometimes I worry he'll get tired of waiting and go off with someone else. Sometimes I think he's frustrated, like I'm letting him down if I don't do it."

"If he pressures you into sex, he's not worth having," Annabelle says.

"I suppose you're right," Bea says. "But still. Did you feel pressured, Annabelle?"

"No," she says. "Not at all."

"Didn't you go out with Kai Nguyen?" I ask. "He was Romeo and you were Juliet, right?" No one could forget those two. They smoldered on the stage so hard, and they were always getting caught making out in the wings before they went on. Mr. Knight had to tell them to knock it off.

"Yep. We lost our virginity on Juliet's balcony." She waits for our reaction, a huge grin on her face.

"Juliet's balcony?" I laugh. "How? It was barely big enough for you, much less two of you!"

159

"We did it standing up, but it wasn't easy. And in the middle of it, part of the scenery came off and we almost fell."

"Oh! I remember that!" Bea says. "Everyone blamed the theater ghost, but it was you?"

"Yep, me and Kai, doing it on the balcony. Losing our virginity." She reaches for another slice. "Man . . . ," she says between bites. "I haven't thought about that guy in a long time. He was really nice."

We sit there quietly, each of us maybe thinking about nice boys and carefree hookups.

TWENTY-THREE

An hour after we eat, I take the second round of pills. I wait thirty minutes and spit the pills out. This time, they've dissolved better.

We all climb into bed, Annabelle in her own and Bea next to me. Three hours later, I take the final four pills. I sit on the bathroom floor with the tablets under my tongue. After thirty minutes, I spit them out. And then I wait. I stare at the shower curtain. It's torn on one side and it hangs from the pole. It reminds me of the torn roof lining in Dean's truck.

I wait.

I pull my knees up and lean my forehead against them. I concentrate hard on my stomach, feeling for the cramps to come, even the slightest twinge.

I check the website again. The abortion is supposed to start within four to six hours after the first dose, sometimes even an hour after. But it can take twelve to fourteen hours after the first dose, so maybe I'm in that group. I'm afraid I'll start bleeding, so I put a bunch of towels under me and lean back against the tub. I think about waking up Bea and Annabelle, but they need to sleep, especially Annabelle.

I put my hands over my stomach. *Go away. Please, go away.*

The minutes turn into hours, and I feel nothing. My body is exhausted, but my mind is racing, so sleep is not an option. Not a single cramp, not nausea, not chills or fever. I don't need the bottle of ibuprofen. The box of maxi pads remains unopened on the bathroom counter. At five in the morning I get up, put on my pajama pants, and go into the bedroom.

"Guys?" I say kind of loudly.

"Everything okay?" Annabelle asks, her voice croaky with sleep.

Bea sits bolt upright.

"Nothing happened."

Annabelle sits up and pushes the blankets away. "What?"

I grab the aspirin bottle off the nightstand and throw it into the trash. "It's only eighty percent effective, and I must be that twenty percent of ineffective. Of course it wouldn't work. Because why would it?"

Annabelle gets out of bed. "Okay, don't panic. So, we wait a while longer—"

Bea runs into the bathroom and comes out with a glass of water. She holds it out to me.

I take the water and sink onto my bed. "It should have happened already. It's not going to work."

"Maybe we should try again," Annabelle says. "Maybe we should get a different brand?"

"I can't! There's a whole thing I have to do. I have to wait for three days before I can try it again. I don't have enough time to wait. I'm already eleven weeks pregnant now, and I can't take the pills after twelve weeks. Meanwhile I'm getting more and more pregnant, and I can't take it anymore!"

"Jesus, Camille, I'm so sorry," Annabelle says. She holds out a tissue, but I don't take it.

"This whole thing has been a waste of time and money and effort. I missed Willow. I probably can't go back to the Globe ever again. I want to throw this glass against the mirror and watch it crack into a million pieces and not give a crap how many years of bad luck I'll get from it."

"Don't do that," Bea says. She takes the water glass from my hand. "Of course you can go back to the Globe again. Mr. Knight will be glad for you to come back."

"No way. I can't show my face there again. I'm the girl who gave up Willow because she was too scared to go. Every single actor at the Globe wants to go to Willow, it's like winning the lottery, and I threw it away. Who does that?" I'm totally babbling but I don't care. It's all piling on me again, that avalanche of shame and despair that no one can help me fix. "What are my parents going to think about me when they hear the entire story? God, it will be the worst thing ever." I double over and clutch my stomach. "It's not fair! It's not fair!"

Annabelle bites her lip. She doesn't say anything else, and that scares me. Annabelle always has an answer for everything, but she doesn't have a plan for this.

"Maybe you aren't pregnant anymore," Bea says. "I've heard of women whose pregnancy disappeared."

"Another podcast?" Annabelle asks.

"No, a TV show."

"Like that would happen to me." I clench my hands so hard, I can feel my nails biting into my palms.

They win—the crisis center people, the judge, the guardian ad litem, the protesters, even that Christian family in the Waffle Factory. They've all won, and I've lost. I imagine how happy they would be if they knew it, their realization that their prayers worked, their judgment worked. *Think you can have sex? Well, think again.*

It feels like a knife in my heart.

"First thing we have to do is see if you're still pregnant. Maybe Bea is right." Annabelle moves into action. She grabs her clothes from the bottom of her bed and starts to get dressed. "Bea, stay here with Camille. I'm going to buy a pregnancy test." Annabelle leaves.

"Maybe it's time to tell your parents." Bea sits on the bed and puts her hand on my back, rubbing in little circles.

Tears gather into my eyes and spill onto my cheeks at the thought of it. I don't bother to wipe them away. I don't have the strength to lift my arms. To pick up my phone. To call my parents.

* * *

When Annabelle returns, I do the pee-on-the-end thing, and Annabelle takes it out of my hand, not caring that my pee is still dripping off it. She watches it for the three full minutes before throwing it in the trash. Her face tells me everything.

I feel hope drain out of me. There's nothing left in me. This is what giving up feels like. An empty feeling, like you could cross a street in the middle of traffic and not care if a bus hits you.

I go into the bathroom and start packing my stuff. Like a robot, I brush my hair. My eyes are bloodshot from crying and lack of sleep.

I take out my phone.

Hi Mom. Call when you get a chance?

I dial the Houston clinic.

"Hi, this is Camille Winchester. I was in there last week for my first appointment. I had an appointment for this Monday, but I had to cancel it. Is it still available?"

"Camille Winchester?" I can hear the woman typing on her computer. "Oh yes. You had your sonogram with Dr. Esperanza. I'm afraid that space is no longer available. I can get you in on her first appointment in two weeks."

"Two weeks? Isn't there anything earlier with another doctor?"

"I'm so sorry, but Dr. Esperanza has to do the procedure, or else you'll have to start over with another doctor. How many weeks pregnant are you?"

"Eleven," I say. "The procedure costs more after twelve weeks, right?"

"I'm afraid so."

I swallow. "Um, how much?"

"The price doubles, I'm afraid. And it's a more complicated procedure. Have you tried New Mexico? There are no age restrictions or waiting periods there."

"No. I didn't know about New Mexico. I didn't know they did that."

"Give me your email address and I'll send you a list."

TWENTY-FOUR

I run out of the bathroom. "New Mexico," I say. I grab my shorts and tank top and pull them on. I search around the room for my phone charger.

"What about it?" Bea says.

"There are no restrictions. No parental permission, no waiting period. Annabelle, can we—"

"Let's do it." Annabelle stands up and starts getting her stuff together.

Bea looks at her phone. "Albuquerque is fourteen hours from here," she says. "That's really far. I don't think . . ."

I grab the pizza box out of the trash and copy the clinic phone numbers down on it.

Annabelle and I start calling. But each clinic we call is

slammed, and each receptionist says the same thing—they are booked with women from Texas.

"I'm looking for an appointment for an abortion," Annabelle says to the third or fourth clinic on her list. She shoots me a thumbs-up. "Yeah," she says to the woman on the phone. "We can do that." She scribbles a date onto the pizza box. She hands the phone to me. "She has some questions for you."

My phone buzzes with another phone call coming through. *Mom* flashes on the screen, and I send her call to voice mail.

I make the appointment for July fifth and hang up the phone. I have enough money. I can do this on my own, just like I wanted to all along.

"Next stop, New Mexico, ladies," Annabelle says. She shoulders her tote bag. "Let's go."

We get in Buzzi and leave Alamo, head north onto the highway, toward New Mexico.

My phone dings. It's my mom. *I tried to call you. Everything okay?*

I pause, my fingers hovering over the keys. For just a second I think about calling her and telling her where we are going and why. But when I imagine her voice on the phone, and how she pauses after she hears something she doesn't like, dread washes over me. I can't do it.

Yep! Just wanted to say hi. So . . . HIIII.

:) Hope you're having fun.

Thanks Mom.

* * *

Annabelle insists she can drive straight through, but Bea and I veto that and decide on ten hours, max. We call ahead to get a motel for tonight to avoid repeating another Boobie Bungalow bungle.

Ten hours doesn't seem that long on the face of it. You can binge-watch a series in ten hours and barely notice. Play practice can last that long. You can sleep for ten hours and wake up feeling really good. But ten hours driving in a car is another thing altogether. Especially for Annabelle, who has to sit in the same position hour after hour. "I'm used to it," she claims. "From flying international. You hunker down and accept your fate."

Bea wants me to sit in the back where I can stretch out and rest, but I want to ride shotgun where the view is better. Where I can see every mile sign, every truck stop, and every billboard as it vanishes behind us.

"I can't believe we have to drive all the way to New Mexico," I say. "Texas is a joke."

"This should have been over and done with for you already, and it isn't fair. It isn't fair that you have to miss out on your future because of one mistake you made in the past. I am so sick of old white dudes telling us what we can and can't do with our bodies. It feels as if I need written permission to live every morning. There shouldn't be a question of who is qualified to make a decision about *your* body. I was a volunteer escort at the clinic in Victorville before it closed, and you wouldn't believe what the women went through. The protesters, first of all. It's beyond scary and humiliating to have to run through a gauntlet of dickheads screaming at you.

"Most of the women at our clinic were low income, mostly African American and Latina, scraping up six hundred bucks for the procedures from God knows where, plus taking time off work, which had to cost them more money. Once our clinic got a bomb threat, so that meant we had to evacuate the clinic, and none of the procedures got done that day. Texas doesn't give two shits about women or the babies they force them to have." Annabelle is talking really loudly. I lower my visor, and in the mirror, I see Bea. She's very pointedly looking at her phone, clearly trying to ignore Annabelle. "Fucking hypocrites. You went to the clinic in Houston, right, Camille?"

At that, Bea glances up, and she and I make eye contact.

"Yeah, I did."

TWENTY-FIVE
JUNE 26

A line of people stand in front of Planned Parenthood holding signs and pictures of aborted fetuses. Some are holding rosaries, their heads bowed.

I make the mistake of looking at one of the protestors, a man about my father's age. He's wearing a T-shirt that says ABORTION IS MURDER.

He holds out a pamphlet. "Jesus loves you, and he doesn't want you to have an abortion. He's given you this child as a gift."

I ignore him and grip the strap of my bag. My heart starts to beat hard, and I want to run away.

Two clinic volunteers dressed in bright pink vests stand between the protesters and me. But that doesn't stop them from yelling at me. "The devil has you in his grasp," one of them shouts. "Those women are his handmaids!"

"Don't worry about them," an escort with long braids says. "They're here all the time."

"Don't let them intimidate you," another volunteer says.

Too late.

I check in, and the receptionist hands me a clipboard with paperwork to fill out. I find a seat toward the back and sit down, tucking my purse under the chair. The girl next to me is talking to her boyfriend, something about getting a pizza tonight. He puts his arm around her and kisses the top of her head.

I look away before they notice me staring.

I fill out the paperwork as fast as I can, worried the nurse will call my name before I'm done. My pen pauses over one question: *How many sexual partners have you had?* I look around the room, wondering how many sexual partners all these people have had.

I hate that phrase *sexual partners*. It sounds like something from the sixties, like the word *lover*. I'm not sure Dean qualifies as a sexual partner, because it only happened once. I write in the number one, cross it out, and then write in one again with a question mark next to it.

I watch patients come into the clinic. Some walk in with their arms crossed tight over their bodies, staring down at the ground like they want to make themselves as small as they can. Some come in defiant, their jaws set and a determined look in their eyes. Most of the women are accompanied by other women, though a few are with guys; one trails behind his girlfriend, his expression sheepish, holding a wad of money in his hand.

People come out of the clinic door clutching small cans of ginger ale and white prescription drug envelopes. Some are crying; some look relieved. Others come out nonchalant, and I have to guess those are the ones here for birth control and not abortions.

Finally, my name is called. The nurse takes me down a hall, and we do the weigh-in—I've gained two more pounds—blood pressure, and temperature thing.

She hands me a plastic cup, and I go into the bathroom and pee in it. I leave it on a little shelf in the bathroom where she told me to, wash my hands, and leave. I feel sorry for the person who has to test those pee cups day in and day out. It must be the grossest job.

Another nurse takes me into a room and has me undress from the waist down. This time I leave on my socks. I hide my underwear inside my jeans pocket.

I sit on the crinkly paper and wrap the paper sheet around me. I wait. The longer I wait, the more nervous I get. I think about the crisis center, and how they made me wait on purpose. I know this is Planned Parenthood and they wouldn't do that, but I can't convince my body. My hands start to sweat and my heart starts in with that pounding.

There's a knock on the door, and a woman in a lab coat comes in. She's reading my file and closes the door with her foot.

She sits on a rolling chair. "Hi, Camille," she says. She holds out her hand and I shake it. "I'm Dr. Esperanza." She wades in right away. "So you probably already know that you're pregnant, and the test does confirm that. You're trying for a judicial bypass?"

"Yes, I've already met with the lawyer Jane's Due Process got for me."

"Okay, so this will be our first appointment together, which will include the Texas-mandated counseling and ultrasound to confirm the pregnancy. Your second will be the actual procedure. Now, have you thought of all your options?"

"I don't want to have it," I say quickly, firmly. "I don't want to talk about my choices. I mean, if that's okay." I try to look Dr. Esperanza in the eye, but I can't. I'm not like those defiant girls in the waiting room. I try to sit up. I try to pretend I am.

She hands me a pink booklet called *A Woman's Right to Know*. "Texas law requires me to present this to you, but I can tell you that it isn't accurate. For instance, the side effects of abortion that they name are the same ones as being pregnant. Look it over because the judge might ask you questions to check you've read it, and then make sure you keep it for your court file."

"Okay," I say, my voice shaking. "Did I fill out the paperwork correctly? I mean, I didn't know what to put for birth control or for that question about sexual partners. I've only been with one guy." I swallow. "Man, I mean. He's not my partner." *Stop talking, Camille!*

"Of course," she says. "Go ahead and lie back, and we'll get started."

The ultrasound is the exact same thing they did at the crisis center so I know what's coming—the cold, hard probe covered in goo. But I'm having a harder time putting it in. It's like my insides have clenched up.

Dr. Esperanza sets her hand on my shoulder, her face kind. "It will be better if you relax. I know that's easier said than done."

I finally get it in, and Dr. Esperanza takes hold of the handle.

Dr. Esperanza is gentle, and I don't feel it sweeping around as much as I did at the crisis center.

"Okay, Camille," says Dr. Esperanza, looking at the screen. "I'm required by Texas law to describe what I see. You don't have to respond. By the measurement from head to rump the fetus is about eleven weeks along, and about an inch and a half in size. I'm going to turn the screen toward you, but it's up to you if you want to look at it."

She turns the screen, and I keep looking at the ceiling. I hear the squeak of the screen as she turns it back toward her and then the hum of the printer. She takes the ultrasound picture and puts it into my file. I remove the probe and take the cloth she hands me. She holds out her hand and helps me sit up. The paper crunches as I scoot back on the table.

"Any questions for me?" she asks.

"Will the abortion hurt?"

"It can be uncomfortable with cramping and bleeding, but we'll prescribe pain medication to make it easier for you."

Suddenly I don't care if the abortion hurts or not. I want this over and done with. I'm sick of thinking about it. I'm sick of it taking over. I want everything back the way it was. I want to stop thinking about what will happen if I let this continue.

TWENTY-SIX
JULY 2

*T*he billboards continue to zip by out the window.

"I had to face the protesters again when I left, but otherwise, the experience wasn't too bad." I turn to look at Bea, who wipes away a tear. Everything that has happened in this car, everything I've told her, is so beyond her comprehension. Not that I'm some expert. But up to this point, the biggest problem she and I have ever had to face is what monologue to use for our auditions. I give her knee a gentle squeeze and turn back around. I start to think about this pregnant girl in my school, Gina Silvestri. She'd walk through the hallways, her book bag pulling her shoulder down, her top pulled tight over her bulging stomach. But her shirts were never long enough, so you could see the naked bottom of her baby bump.

"Do you remember Gina Silvestri?" I ask Annabelle.

She shakes her head. "I don't think so."

"I do," Bea says. "I had English lit with her. She sat way in the back and hardly ever raised her hand."

"She had a baby last winter. Guys treated her like shit when she was pregnant, asking her what she was going to do now that she couldn't go to college, and how did it feel to have the rest of your life ruined at sixteen; they were even calling her 'baby mama.' She'd pretend like she didn't hear them, but her face would turn bright red. Sometimes she looked like she was going to cry. Some people didn't look at her or talk to her. It was like her pregnancy would rub off on them if they did."

"I hate that school." Annabelle turns the radio knob until she lands on a station.

"I felt sorry for her," Bea says.

"Not everyone made fun of her, but no one defended her. Not even the teachers—they let it all happen."

Annabelle makes a face. "It's, like, why bother helping someone who decided to make the world's worst choice—the choice to get knocked up and display it for all the world to see? There's no way to win. You're a monster if you get an abortion, a slut if you had sex, a moron if you decide to keep the baby. God, she must have been so lonely."

"The boys, the ones who called her Juno—I know for a fact that they'd all done it. But who are the ones who get shamed? Not them."

"I know," Annabelle says.

"I should have defended her," I say. I lean my head against the dirty window. It's cold from the AC, and I can feel the road vibrating through the glass.

"You didn't know her, Camille," Bea says. "Don't feel bad. I didn't defend her, either."

"Still," I say. I decide then and there that I won't let a bunch of assholes bully a girl like Gina again. I imagine me in Annabelle's Wendy shirt, stomping up to the boys and getting right in their faces, not caring if they're embarrassed or humiliated, or whatever. I won't care if they decide to take their revenge on me either because after what's happened this summer, I can take it. And what's more, I won't give a single fuck.

"Did she keep the baby or put it up for adoption?" Annabelle asks.

"She kept it," Bea says. "A girl. Her family moved away right after."

"What do you think it feels like to be pregnant?" I ask Annabelle. "I mean, not when it's early. Like . . . later, when you can feel the baby kick and all that?"

"Awful," Annabelle says. "I don't want to have kids. I bet it feels like your body's been hijacked."

"I bet it feels magical," Bea says. "To think you can make another person inside your own body. I can't wait to have kids. I'll have a dozen if I can afford it."

"How about you, Camille?" Annabelle looks at me. "Do you think you'll have children someday?"

I don't reply right away because I don't have an answer. "I'm not sure," I finally say. "I suppose I should know, especially now, but I just don't."

We only stop for bathroom breaks and to grab coffee and Sprite and Dunkaroos when we see them. After exactly ten hours driving, we force Annabelle to stop at our motel. We have dinner at the restaurant across the street, and then fall into bed, exhausted.

We wake up as soon as the sun rises, still groggy with sleep. We use the shower and have the free breakfast in the lobby—cornflakes in foam cups and cold bagels with a square of fake cream cheese on top. We chase it all down with tiny cups of orange juice. Bea watches while Annabelle gets her three morning coffees in.

We're halfway to the car when Annabelle's phone rings. She pulls it out of her pocket, looks at it, and stops in her tracks. The bag filled with our lunch—granola bars, sodas, and cheese sticks—drops from her hand.

"You okay?" I ask.

She ignores me and answers her phone. "Hello? Yes, this is her. Okay. Um . . ." She glances at us. "Hold on." Annabelle hands me the keys and walks away, leaving the bag on the ground. I pick it up and walk to Buzzi.

"What do you think is going on?" Bea asks.

I shrug.

Annabelle stares at a field filled with several oil derricks, their tops pumping up and down. She nods and walks back and forth along the field in a tight line, scrubbing at her eyes. A minute later, she hangs up and sits on the dusty ground cross-legged. Her shoulders are shaking. I can hear her crying.

I start to walk over to her, but then I stop. Bea looks at me, concerned.

"She's crying," I say. "I don't know what to do."

"Should we go over there?"

"I don't know."

Bea gets in the car, but I wait. Annabelle's coming back now. Her eyes are puffy and her face streaked with tears. She gets into the car and slams the door. I get in and hand her the keys. She takes them without speaking.

I put my hand on her arm, but she shakes me off and starts the car. "What's wrong?" I ask her. She ignores me again and pulls out of the truck stop.

She snaps on the radio, fiddling with the dial to find something she likes. Songs judder past, running into one another, as she rolls the dial over and over. Back and forth, back and forth. Finally she settles on a country station, something she hates.

"Do you want to talk? I mean, I'm here for you if you want to talk about that phone—"

"No," she says. "Please, Camille. I don't." Her breath hitches. "I don't."

"I'm here if you want to talk."

"I know," she says. She blinks back tears. "I know."

The windows are down, and the smell of cow manure streaming into the car is so strong, my eyes start to water. I roll my window up, but Annabelle punches the button on her side, and the window rolls down again. I lay my finger on the metal tab of the window control. Annabelle gives me the side-eye, and I take my finger away.

Annabelle turns the dial on the radio. It's the Talking Heads song "Road to Nowhere." The group sings about how they're not little children and that they know what they want. I think about my life and how I got here, and a giant anvil of sadness falls on me. I'm on the road to nowhere.

Bea slumps down and puts her feet on the back of the seat.

"Can you take your feet down?" Annabelle says.

Bea yanks her feet down. "What is with you?" She starts to cry.

"Why are you crying?" Annabelle asks.

"What if Camille is killing a baby?" she blurts out.

Annabelle jerks the steering wheel and stamps on the brake, and the car comes to a screeching halt on the shoulder. "Jesus, Annabelle!" I shout. Nausea floods over me. I unbuckle my seat belt, open the door, and puke all over a tiny cactus. My eyes water with the effort. Poor cactus. The thought of the cactus dying because of me makes me start to cry. I puke and cry. Cry and puke. I hear the driver's side door open, and Annabelle is there. She pats my back.

I hear the crunch of gravel, and Bea kneels down beside me. "I'm sorry, Camille. I didn't mean to upset you."

"What did you think that little comment would do?" Annabelle yells. She kicks some gravel. "Make her happy?"

"I didn't mean it! It just slipped out." Bea stands up.

"Pretty princess didn't mean this, didn't mean that. Words hurt, Bea, especially when someone is going through a hard time. Get out of your bubble, why don't you?"

"You're *not* Camille's friend, I am! I think I know what's best for her. You're so arrogant, Annabelle." Bea flings out her arms. "Miss Perfect Actress, Mr. Knight's pet, England's answer to Shakespeare!"

Annabelle sticks up her middle finger and stomps off. She stops by a sign advertising thirty-six-ounce steaks at Billy Bob's. Billy Bob is dressed in a red check shirt with a bandanna stuffed in the neck of his shirt. He holds a knife in one hand and a fork in the other, grinning down at a huge lump of beef.

The sight of that steak makes me gag, and my stomach rolls again. I start to tell them to stop it when Annabelle turns around and comes back. "So you want to know something, Bea. Well, here's one: I'm no Miss Perfect Actress. That phone call before? That was RADA telling me not to come back. I'll never be an actor, I'm not cut out for it, and I knew it. I'm quitting acting. How about that?"

I stare at Annabelle. "You can't be serious."

She makes a sweeping gesture. "Like I made that up."

"Why would they do that?" Bea asks. "You're really good. Your name is painted on Mr. Knight's Masters of Their Fates wall. Why would RADA kick you out? It doesn't make sense."

"The other students are better, okay? It's one thing to be the best at the Globe and another to be the best in England. God, not even the best, just good enough would have been fine. I sounded like an idiot next to them. I don't know what I'm doing;

my grades suck. The director of RADA hauled me into her office and asked why I was there. She told me to go home for the summer and think about it. Everyone else headed off to the summer program or up to Stratford-upon-Avon to a special Shakespeare study course. And I came home to Johnson Creek, Texas, to work in the janky pharmacy off the highway."

"Don't listen to her, Annabelle," I say. "You're amazing!"

"Who should I listen to?" She scrubs her eyes. "I don't know what else to do. What else to be."

She looks out across the desert. "I knew I couldn't handle it there. Everything about it scared me. The Underground terrified me, and I spent most of my travel money on cabs. It's just . . ." Annabelle shakes her head. "I'm sick of this shit." She picks up a rock and flings it at the sign. It soars through the air and hits Billy Bob right on the head. "Fuck you, Billy Bob!"

I throw my bottle on the ground; it bursts open and water gushes out. I pick up a rock. "I'm so tired of people judging," I say. "How is it selfish to want a life? How is it selfish to not want to be a mother at seventeen?" I throw the rock. "Fuck you, Billy Bob!"

Bea picks up a rock next to me. "I'm tired of being perfect, of worrying about how my parents see me, how my church sees me. Fuck you, Billy Bob!" She hurls the rock at the sign.

Annabelle picks up another rock. "Fuck you, dudes who ran us off the road!"

"Fuck you, crisis center!" I shout.

"Eat shit, asshole judge!" Annabelle yells as she whips another rock.

We look at Bea to see what she has next. "I, uh, can't think of anyone else I'm mad at," she says. But she picks up a rock and hucks it at the billboard.

We fling rock after rock until Billy Bob's face is streaked in pink dust. Until our arms are tired and our hands are filthy, until we are breathless, until we run out of rocks to throw.

"Jeez Louise," Bea says. Her face is smudged with dirt, and her sundress is streaked with red dust.

Annabelle straightens up and looks toward the road. Her smile fades.

Coming toward us are two police officers.

"Oh no," Bea says.

"You girls okay?" one of the troopers asks. "You seem to be letting off some steam with that sign there."

We exchange glances, and Bea speaks up before Annabelle or I can. "Our friend got carsick." She waves toward the cactus I've puked on. One of the cops' gazes follows her hand, and he takes a step back.

"Throwing rocks at a billboard helps with that?"

"I'm sorry, Officer. We had a bad day, and we kind of lost it."

He sighs and looks at the sign. "Well, I've seen old Billy Bob look worse on a Saturday night. That dirt will come off next rain."

The older trooper jumps in, his voice gruff. "All the same, I need your licenses, ladies, and the car registration."

We give them our licenses, and the older trooper watches as Annabelle opens her glove box. An avalanche of CDs and fast food napkins pour out. She picks out her registration and hands it to him.

He takes them and returns to the car, leaving the younger trooper to keep an eye on us.

"Going far?" he asks, making the smallest of small talk.

"New Mexico," Annabelle says.

"For Fourth of July," Bea blurts out.

"My aunt Pam lives there," I say, even though my aunt Pam moved to Indiana years ago. "We're staying with her."

Minutes later, the older trooper comes walking back, fast. "Which one of you is Annabelle Ponsonby?"

Annabelle holds up her hand.

"Hands on the car, miss," he says.

"What? Why?" she asks.

"Hands on the car," he says. "Don't make me ask you again."

"Wait!" I say. "What's happening?"

Annabelle sets her palms on the car's hood, and the officer pulls his handcuffs out of his belt. "You have the right to remain silent," he says, pulling one arm back and then the other, clicking the handcuffs. "There's a bench warrant out for your arrest."

"For what?" Annabelle asks.

"Theft."

"I've never stolen anything!" she says, her voice high and wobbly.

"The dispatch says differently. Apparently you shoplifted something from a pharmacy? Any of that ring a bell?" The way he says it is less like a question than a statement. He starts moving toward his car, dragging her a little when she tries to dig her heels in. The pink Panhandle dirt rises in little puffs as she shuffles her feet.

The cop behind them snaps his fingers. "Let's go, let's go," he says. "You don't want to add resisting arrest to the list, now do you?"

"Hey, wait," I say. "Where are you taking her?"

"This has to be a mistake," Bea pipes up. "Can you look again? Maybe there's another Annabelle Ponsonby. Honestly, Officer, she's a good person."

But I know there is no mistake. The pregnancy test. She stole it. That's why Annabelle didn't want money for it. I can picture her now, unlocking the box with her employee key, taking out the pregnancy test, and stomping out of the store and into the night.

She did that for me. She shoplifted so that I could have the test.

She's going to jail because of me.

"County jail in Louiston," the younger trooper says.

They put Annabelle in the back seat; the cops climb in, the car pulls onto the highway and drives past me. I can't see Annabelle through the tinted windows.

Bea and I stand there. Left behind in the Panhandle without Annabelle and with a car we can't drive.

TWENTY-SEVEN

We run to Buzzi, and I jump in the driver's side. Bea climbs into the passenger side. Keys, keys . . . I see them dangling from the ignition.

"How did Annabelle do this?" I ask. "Did you watch her?"

"Um, she put her foot on that pedal to the left and then moved the stick?" Bea says. "I think?"

"Moved the stick how?"

Bea shrugs. "I don't know."

I turn the ignition, but the car jerks and stalls. "I can't even turn this thing on!"

"Maybe you push on that pedal first?" Bea points to the floor. "Hang on. I'm asking Google." Bea taps in *How to drive a manual car*. "Okay, I'm going to read this out to you, you ready? That pedal on the end is called the clutch."

"The clutch. Got it."

"You step on that when you shift. Push it all the way to the floor, and at the same time, hit the accelerator. You listen to the engine. When you hear it revving, shift into a higher gear."

I start the car. But I can't get the hang of using the clutch and the accelerator at the same time. I stall the car three times in a row.

"Shit, shit! I can't do this." I bang the steering wheel with my palms.

"Hey! If you can stand on a stage in front of a ton of people, you can drive a stick! People do this all the time."

My shoulders relax a little. "You're right."

"Listen to me and do exactly what I tell you." Bea turns around and scans the road. "The road is clear. Let's try merging on. When you let the clutch out, hit the accelerator, pick up speed on the side of the road, and then merge on. I'll tell you when to shift, okay?"

I step on the clutch, put the car into first, let the clutch out, and stamp on the accelerator. The car bucks forward and I'm moving.

"Shift!" Bea yells. "Clutch in and hit second!"

I do it, the car jolts forward, and the engine revs. I shift into third and then fourth.

I head out onto the highway, engine whining.

"Fifth!"

I fiddle with the stick. "Where is fifth?"

"Move your hand." She looks at the stick shift. "Um. Up and over to the right."

I shove the stick to the right and the engine calms down.

"Woo!" Bea says. "You're doing it!"

I grin, but I don't respond because I'm terrified. Bea and I both sit perched forward. I'm clutching the steering wheel so hard, my hands ache. I stare out at the road through the bug-splattered windshield.

Bea guides me to Louiston Police Department. There are three stoplights before the station. I stall the car at two of the stoplights. The driver of a red jacked-up truck leans on the horn in one long honk until I get the car going again. He passes me and mouths *asshole* and glares. If my hands hadn't been occupied by trying to shift and steer at the same time, I might have flipped him off, two handed, Beatrice Delgado style.

I find the police department and park in front.

"Wait," I say. I rummage around inside Annabelle's pack, find her Wendy shirt, and pull it on over my tank top. We need a little of Wendy Davis's courage right now.

A cluster of people sit in chairs in the middle of the room, but Annabelle isn't among them. There isn't a big desk with a policeman sitting behind it, like you see in the movies. I don't know where to go, so I ask a man staring at his phone if he knows who I can ask. Without taking his eyes off his phone, he points to the back of the room. Bea and I go over and step up to a glass window. A bored-looking police officer sits behind it. I give him Annabelle's name. The police officer taps it into his computer.

"Annabelle Ponsonby?" His voice is made tinny by the microphone.

"That's her," Bea says. "She didn't do anything—"

He gets up, his gun belt creaking, and leaves his desk without saying anything. We stand at the window waiting and waiting. I'm about to tell Bea let's go sit in the chairs when he comes back.

"None of the judges are in today since it's a holiday, but the jail is overcrowded with early Fourth of July drunks, so we got a judge to hold a video court." He looks at the clock. "In about three hours."

"Three hours?"

"That's what I said." He points to the chairs. "You can wait over there or come back. Up to you." He turns back to his computer.

"Can I talk to her?"

"Only if she calls you."

"What if the judge says she's guilty?"

The police officer sighs. "Texas law, less than a fifty-dollar theft is a class C misdemeanor, three-hunerd-dollar fine. Up to four hunerd and ninety-nine dollars is a class B misdemeanor. That comes with a side of four months in jail and a two-thousand-dollar fine."

"It didn't cost much," I say. "Probably only ten dollars."

"Doesn't matter what it is," he says slowly and loudly, as though I were a little kid without the ability to comprehend simple sentences. "It can be two cents, for all the law cares. Shoplifting is shoplifting. Got it?"

"What if she can't pay the fine?" Bea puts in.

"Then she sits in jail until she can."

"But that's not right—"

The police officer scowls. "Look, ladies. Do I look like a politician? They make the laws. Not me. Take it up with your congressmen. Your friend broke the law, and she has to pay the consequences. Now take a seat or leave."

We return to the chairs and sit in the two remaining empty seats. Mine is broken, and it wobbles when I sit down. A woman sitting next to me is crying, mouth open and tears streaming down her cheeks. She's not even trying to hide it.

A woman wearing ripped-up jeans and dollar store flip-flops sits across from me, her arms folded. Her T-shirt says COME CLASSY, LEAVE TRASHY. She leans forward and stares at me. "Got any money?" she asks. "I wanna Coke."

"I'm sorry. I don't," I say.

Bea clutches her purse to her chest.

"You look like you got at least a dollar." Her eyes narrow. "You lyin'."

If a dollar is all it takes to get her to leave me alone, I'll give it to her. I grab my purse and take out a dollar. She snatches it out of my hand and heads over to the soda machine.

"She wants a Coke, all right," a man in a red baseball cap says, looking up from his magazine. "Cocaine. Or maybe crack. You shouldn't've given her money. Now she'll pester the life out of you for more. Whenever people ask me for money, I tell them go work at McDonald's. As long as they can say 'you want fries with that?' they can work, same as I do. I work hard for my money—"

I glance at Bea. We stand up and leave the station and go sit in Buzzi.

A few minutes later my phone rings.

"This is a call from an inmate at Louiston Detention Center," an automated voice says when I answer the call. "Press one to accept the charges. This call will be recorded."

I press one and put the phone on speaker.

"Camille?" It's Annabelle. She sounds panicked, her voice high and thin.

"Annabelle?"

"That asshole pharmacist put a warrant out for my arrest. I have to see a judge! Where are you? Are you still by the side of the road?"

"We're here. I talked to the police officer and he said the least it will be is three hundred dollars."

Annabelle is silent for a moment. "I don't have three hundred dollars. I have maybe fifty on me and not much in my bank account."

"I have money," I say.

"No way! You need that, Camille. If you figured out how to drive my car, go to New Mexico without me. I'll figure something else out." Her voice catches.

"I'm not leaving you here," I say.

The automatic voice cuts in. "One minute remaining."

"Shit," Annabelle says.

"Are you all right in there?"

"Yeah. There's a bunch of us. We're all sitting on a bench in a room that's hot, and there aren't any windows. God, Camille, what if they put me in jail?"

"They won't—"

The automated voice comes in and the phone cuts out.

I can't go. I can't leave her in jail like that.

"I don't know what to do," I tell Bea. "We can't leave Annabelle to rot in jail with no way to get out. She doesn't have anyone else to help her. What kind of person abandons her friend?"

Bea's face flushes.

"Oh . . . no, no, no. Bea, I didn't mean you."

"I know you didn't." Bea fiddles with the strap on her purse. "I'm sorry I said that, Camille," Bea says. "About killing a baby. I shouldn't have. I truly didn't come on this trip to stop you. It was as if everything that my parents and church friends have been saying for years came flying out of my mouth and I couldn't stop it. I saw the look in your eyes and wanted to just shut up, but I couldn't."

"I know this must be hard for you, Bea, but you have to accept that it's my decision and one that I have to make about my own body."

"I know. You're right. You're my best friend, and more than that, what kind of person would I be if I turned my back on someone who needed help? Even if the help is more about support than guidance?"

"Hate the sin, love the sinner?"

"I fucking hate that saying," Bea says.

"You said fuck. Again!" I say, laughing.

"I think I love that word," she says. "It's so . . . perfect."

"It kind of is," I say.

"Look, I don't have another hundred-dollars-behind-Jesus. But . . ." Bea takes out her wallet and counts her money. "I have seventy-six dollars." She dumps her wallet on her lap and sorts through movie ticket stubs, a single gold earring, a hair band, and a pile of change. "Looks like eighty-five cents."

"I have seven hundred and change."

"Gosh, that's a lot of money."

"It's the money I saved for Willow and what's left of my latest Iggy's paycheck."

"I'm sorry, Camille. This whole thing stinks. You don't deserve any of this."

"Yeah, well, at least I have it. So we have a little under eight hundred bucks. And I need six for the procedure, which means we don't have enough to bail out Annabelle." My shoulders slump.

"We need money to get to New Mexico and back home, too," Bea says. "And we need a hotel for at least one night. You won't want to go home straight after the . . ." She swallows.

"You're right." I sit back in my seat. "Okay, think, Bea."

"I could ask Mateo for the money, but I doubt he has that much."

I shake my head. "Remember, the fewer people we drag into this, the better. Besides, he's saving up for a car."

She sighs. "And my parents are out for sure."

"How can we get some money quick?" I ask. "Think."

"Too bad we can't have a bake sale. Our church gets tons of money whenever we have those."

I give her a look. "People would love that. Money for a poor pregnant girl and a jailbird." I think for a second. "Actually, your bake sale idea isn't all that kooky."

"Where will we bake things, though?"

"I don't mean baking. We could do a flash play, like how we do for the Globe. " Every year at the county fair, Mr. Knight takes a bunch of us, and we act out a scene from a play we're doing. People look forward to seeing those every year.

"We could do that!" Bea bounces in her seat. "We could do that easy!"

"We're four hours from Albuquerque, and it's bound to be busy on the Fourth of July. If we put out a bucket or something, people will give money, I'm sure they will."

"How will it work, though? Mr. Knight had a big group, and people liked the surprise of seeing who was going to turn into a character. We have to get their attention somehow."

"That's true. What if we start out having an argument, like the modern version of the scene, and then switch into Shakespeare?"

"There's a ton of fights in Shakespeare we could do," Bea says. "But I think we should do a comedy. How about *The Taming of the Shrew*? The one with Katherine, Bianca, and Baptista. That one's really funny, and we've done the scene together."

"It's too short, though."

We throw out a few more ideas—*As You Like It*, *The Comedy of Errors*, *The Merry Wives of Windsor*. It feels good to talk about acting instead of the abortion. And the more we talk, the more we get into the idea.

"We did *Midsummer* a couple of years ago," I say. "There's

that scene between Helena and Hermia. It's really funny. People loved it."

"We had small parts, though. I was Cobweb and you were Mustardseed. Annabelle was Hermia."

"I was swing, though, for Helena, remember?"

"Oh!" Bea says. "That's right."

"There's a small line from Lysander. You could do that."

"Get ye gone, dwarf!" she says. "That one?"

"So it's a plan, then?"

"It's a plan."

The judge fines Annabelle three hundred dollars for the misdemeanor plus twenty-five for the pregnancy test. I pay the fine, but the prison is so crowded, it takes another hour for them to process her paperwork. Finally, people start trickling out of the jail. The man with the magazine is paired with his son, who is about twenty. The man hits him over the head with a rolled-up magazine and swears at him. The crying woman has a husband who doesn't look at her. He storms out of the station while she follows behind, staring at the floor. No one comes out for the woman who begged me for a dollar. She swears, gets up, and leaves. Finally, Annabelle comes out holding a plastic bag that says PRISONER'S BELONGINGS. I can see her purse and phone inside it.

"Oh my god, Annabelle." I rush forward and hug her. "Are you hungry?"

"Starving," Annabelle says. She notices my shirt then. "You brought Wendy with you." She smiles.

* * *

Annabelle drags her fries through a puddle of ketchup. "A flash play?" she asks.

"Yeah," Bea says. "We did the math, and we need some money to cover the, uh, you know—"

"Abortion," Annabelle says.

"—that, plus some money to get home."

"You already know the part," I say. "You were the best Hermia."

"I don't think I can do it," she says. "We have to figure something else out."

Bea and I exchange glances. "We thought you'd love the idea," Bea says.

Annabelle shakes her head. "No, I mean, I don't think I can do it. Physically do it. In England, I sort of got in my head. It got so bad that whenever I put a foot onstage I'd freeze up. I literally couldn't speak."

"Maybe you could be Hermia, Bea," I say.

"I don't know. That's a lot of lines to learn."

I find the lines on my phone, and Bea and I lean over it. Annabelle eats her cheeseburger and doesn't say anything.

Bea shakes her head. "I don't know."

"Try it," I say. "Hermia begins. You juggler!" I prompt.

"You canker-blossom!" Bea says, picking up the line. "You thief of love! What, have you . . . have you . . . uh . . ." She tries to find her spot on the phone.

"Come by night and stol'n my love's heart from him?" Annabelle says.

"Have you no modesty, no maiden shame," I continue with Helena's part. "No touch of bashfulness? What, will you tear impatient answers from my gentle tongue? Fie, fie! You counterfeit, you puppet, you!"

"Puppet?" Bea says. "Why so?—Ay, that way goes the game. Now I perceive that she . . . that she . . ." Bea looks at Annabelle.

". . . hath made compare between our statures!"

Annabelle continues with the monologue, all from memory, from a role she played years ago. She's so good. Annabelle is so damn good! When she's done with the monologue, she lets out a breath and sits back in the booth.

"Wow," Bea says.

"I thought you said you froze up. That didn't look like freezing to me," I say.

"You should do it, Annabelle," Bea says. "We're not going to get any money at all if I do it."

Annabelle sighs. "Okay. I'll do it. Just this once."

I'm hoping it won't be just once. Annabelle is too good to give up on acting.

We watch from our booth as the sun starts to set. A minivan pulls up, and a bunch of kids pour out, chattering and laughing, the boys pushing one another. They come into the restaurant and the adults attempt to get them in line.

"They have no idea what's ahead of them," Annabelle says, nodding toward the kids. She sucks the last bit of Coke from her cup; her straw burbles and a little boy turns to look. He sticks his tongue out and does a goofy dance.

"Well, maybe that kid does," I say, and Annabelle laughs.

We leave the restaurant, but we're not ready to get back on the highway. We sit on Buzzi's hood and lean against the windshield.

"What do you want to be when you grow up?" Bea asks.

"Mr. Rogers," Annabelle says.

"Love him," I say.

"Be serious," Bea insists. "What do you want from your life? I feel like I change my mind all the time, and that can't be good. I should have settled on something by now."

"Same," Annabelle says. "I was so sure I wanted to be an actor and there was nothing else, but that can't be true. There has to be more to me, right?"

"I don't know who I'll be after all this," I say. "How do you deal with awful things that happen? How do you forget them?"

I can feel Annabelle shrug. "I wish I knew. I'm not sure how I can deal with being dumped by RADA, or telling Mr. Knight and my parents."

"My pastor says you can't forget bad stuff, but you learn to carry it. I imagine it's like a backpack; you stick all the junk in there and go on. Heavy things make you stronger." She pauses. "That's dumb, right?"

"I think it's perfect," Annabelle says.

"I read this quote from Virginia Woolf once, about how the future is dark and how she thinks that's the best thing the future can be; that we can't know how our actions can affect it, and how that's good; otherwise we'd lose hope," I say. "But I wish the future weren't dark. I wish it were, like, full of light, so I could see what was ahead of me."

"Me too," Annabelle says.

"Me three," Bea says.

We all hold hands. Stars now fill the sky. I've never seen so many stars in my life.

"The stars at night are big and bright," Annabelle sings softly.

"Deep in the heart of Texas," Bea and I sing.

"And that is why we aren't musical theater actors," I say.

TWENTY-EIGHT

Old Town in Albuquerque is no Holler Up. Talk about jacked for Fourth of July. As soon as we step foot in the town square, we're hit with a holiday bomb. Bright-colored decorations, lights in the trees, and costumed people mix together in a summer kaleidoscope. We'd reached New Mexico last night and stayed in the first motel we found off the interstate. We've been practicing since breakfast, going over our lines until we have them down perfectly. It's lunchtime now, and the plaza is packed with people standing shoulder to shoulder. Normally I hate crowds, but everyone is so happy and joyful that I want to dive in the middle of it and crowd surf.

"Where should we start?" Annabelle asks.

"By that old mission church over there?" I say. "It looks really busy." The crowd's energy has rubbed off on me, and I can't wait to get started on our flash play.

"Wait," Bea says. "Before we start, I have something." She takes a little paper bag out of her purse. "I got these at the Waffle Factory. I meant to give them to you both there, but that family came in . . . and well, it didn't seem right. But now it does." She takes out three matching silver bracelets, each hung with Texas charms—the Texas flag, the bluebonnet, the western boot, the cactus, and the mockingbird. She hands one to me and one to Annabelle. "You don't have to wear them." Her cheeks blush. "Maybe they're babyish. I don't know."

Annabelle puts hers on right away. "If it's babyish to wear a charm bracelet from Beatrice Delgado, then call me a baby."

"Same," I say, putting mine on, too. I hold my hand out. "Hey, let's have the best performance ever."

Annabelle puts her hand on top of mine. "Best performance," she says.

Bea puts hers in.

Our hands stacked one upon the other, I hold up my phone and snap a photo, but I don't put it on Instagram. I don't need to share it with anybody.

We merge into the crush of people and follow the signs to the eighteenth-century San Felipe de Neri church. There are other street performers along the way—dancers, singers, puppeteers, and even a magician. Each of them has a bucket out for tips, and I see people tossing money in. When we reach the church, the crowds are even bigger. The stone-paved square in front of it is crammed with people.

Annabelle is shifting from foot to foot, her eyes glittering and a wide smile on her face. That's the way she always looked before she headed onstage.

"You and Bea go over to that tree, and I'll ambush you there."

They thread their way through the crowd and stop in front of the tree and next to an older man in a button-up shirt with a camera hanging from his neck. A lady in a matching button-up stands next to him. Bea and Annabelle hold hands.

I wipe my sweaty hands on my pants, take a deep breath, and step out onto the square. "Yo, Helena," I shout.

Annabelle looks up. She drops Bea's hand and steps away from her. "Hermia. What's up?"

"I'll tell you what's up. So . . . what kind of friend steals her boyfriend?" I point at Bea.

Annabelle scrunches her face. "Huh?"

And it's on. It's me and Annabelle and Bea and nothing else matters. It's like we're back at the Globe.

We launch into the modern *Midsummer Night's Dream* we created, about a failing friendship, where two girls fight each other over a boy. We argue, we fight; we startle people into stopping and watching.

"You are such a bitch! And the worst friend ever." I give Annabelle a little shove.

The couple next to the tree exchange looks. "Take it easy, girls," the man says. "We're all friends here."

"Have you no modesty, no maiden shame, no touch of bashfulness?" Annabelle says, switching into the actual play.

The man begins to laugh. "Okay, I see what's going on now!"

"Is this one of those flash things?" the wife asks Bea, but Bea is Lysander now and doesn't hear her.

"Puppet?" I take a step back, hurt. "Why so? Ay, that way goes the game." I turn toward the crowd. Several people start to laugh and applaud. "How low am I, thou painted maypole?" I stamp my foot. "Speak. How low am I? I am not yet so low but that my nails can reach unto thine eyes." I run at her, my hands outstretched.

Annabelle shrieks and hides behind Bea.

"I pray you, though you mock me, sir, do let her not hurt me," Annabelle says, cowering behind Bea. "I was never cursed. I have no gift at all in shrewishness. I am a right maid for my cowardice. Let her not strike me. You perhaps may think, because she is something lower than myself, that I can match her."

She exaggerates every word, making the line even more comical. I want to laugh along with the audience. Annabelle is so natural, so good, and acting with her feels so easy. Nothing is in our way. It's why I love acting so much.

"Lower? Hark, again!" I rush Annabelle, and we run in a little circle around Bea.

"Good Hermia, do not be so bitter with me." Annabelle pumps her arms ridiculously, as we chase each other around. The crowd laughs. "I evermore did love you, Hermia," she says. Annabelle stops running and takes a step toward me, her arms stretched out, blinking innocently. "Let me go. You see how simple and fond I am."

I stretch my arms out like I'm going to hug her, a dopey

expression on my face. But as she leans forward for the hug, I put my hand on her forehead and shove. "Who is't that hinders you?"

Annabelle takes a few comical steps back and grabs her forehead. "A foolish heart, that I leave here behind!"

"What, with Lysander?"

"With Demetrius." Annabelle pulls a teenage boy out of the crowd. His friends whoop and laugh. "Oh, when Hermia is angry, she is keen and shrewd!" She leans her head against his. "She was a vixen when she went to school. And though she be but little, she is fierce."

"Little again? Nothing but low and little, why will you suffer her to flout me thus? Let me come to her!"

Annabelle screams and runs into the crowd. "I will not trust you," she calls out. "I, nor longer stay in your curst company. Your hands than mine are quicker for a fray. My legs are longer, though, to run away."

"Get ye gone, dwarf!" Bea shouts out her line.

I chase after Annabelle, weaving my way through the people. I never want the scene to end. I never want this feeling to go away.

We repeat our flash play under a sprawling tree in front of a line of restaurants. We collect three hundred twenty-one bucks and fifty-two cents total. With the money we already have, it's more than enough to cover the cost of my abortion and get us home.

We buy a plate of Navajo fry bread with our earnings and sit at a table cramming the food into our mouths like we've never eaten.

"Oh my god, this is so good," Annabelle says. Sauce drips down her chin, but she doesn't wipe it off.

I lick sauce off my fingers. "You know what? This is our first meal as professional actors. From our first wages."

Bea pauses, her plastic fork halfway to her mouth. "You're right! I never thought about that." She shovels a piece of fry bread into her mouth. "I like it."

"Me too," I say.

"So I did a lot of thinking in the slammer," Annabelle says, wiping her fingers.

"The hoosegow," Bea says.

"Club fed," I say.

"I've decided I'm going to Chicago. You remember Georgia? From the Globe?"

"Yeah."

"I'm going to ask her if I can crash on her sofa for a while. Chicago is great for theaters and improv. I can get a job as a server until I figure out what I want to do. I don't think I'm ready to give up acting just yet. But I'm not going to go unless you promise me you won't give up acting, either."

"I don't know," I say. "I'm the girl who gave up Willow and the cute French guy. How can I get out from under that?"

"You can't give up the Globe," Bea says. "You can't care what people think about you."

"You can pick up and start again," Annabelle says. "Get your ass back there, hold your head high. Take your place again." Chunks of chicken and tomatoes fall off the top of her bread. She looks calm. She looks like the old Annabelle, full of confidence. I want to look that way, too.

"I think you're right."

"Yeah," she says. "I think so, too."

Darkness falls, and Old Town turns bright with lights and Mexican luminarias. A western swing band begins to play on a nearby stage, and fireworks light up the sky. We dump our plates in the trash, hold hands, and run into the crowd, making our way to the front, jumping up and down, dancing and singing along with the crowd. None of us know the lyrics so we make up our own. A group of people near the stage start their own flash performance, dancing the western two-step in perfect choreography.

A cowboy dressed in jeans and a gingham shirt comes over to me. "Would you like to dance?" he asks me. He's cute, with a little gap between his teeth when he smiles. He takes his hat off when he talks to us, and there's a rim around his hair where his hat squashed it down.

Bea pokes me in the arm and grins.

"No, thank you," I say. "I'm dancing with my friends."

He doesn't get angry. He doesn't try to convince me to change my mind. He puts his hat back on. "You ladies have a good night now." He smiles and walks off.

*   *   *

Around midnight, we head back to our motel. Annabelle flops facedown on one of the beds and falls asleep. I take off her shoes and pull the blanket over her. I put a bottle of water on the bedside next to her in case she wakes up thirsty in the night.

Bea crawls into the other bed. "Oh my gosh, I am so tired. You coming to bed?"

"I think I'm going to take a shower, but you go to sleep."

"Okay, sweetie. Sorry if I mumble in my sleep."

"You *always* mumble in your sleep."

"I know, and I'm sorry." She gives me a smile and lies down.

I take a shower and put on my pajamas. I'm so tired that I can't wind down enough to sleep. I lie on my bed and try to listen to a podcast on my phone through my headphones, but I can't concentrate on it. Only a few more hours until I'm not pregnant anymore.

I put my hands over my stomach and remember that ultrasound and think about the little white speck that's grown in the past eleven weeks.

I'm not sure if I believe in God, but I do believe in souls, and I don't think you can kill a soul.

I get up and sit down at the desk, where there's a small pad of paper and a pen.

Dear Soul,

I hope you understand why I can't give you life. I have to find my own life before I can give one to you. I hope you find someone else who wants you and will love you

like you deserve. If you want to wait around, I hope
you'll return to me one day when I'm ready for you. I
hope to meet you someday.

Love, Camille

I find a pack of matches in the desk drawer. I light the paper and drop it into the trash can. The paper catches, my words disappearing into smoke and ashes. And I say goodbye.

TWENTY-NINE

There are three protesters outside the women's clinic. One leans against a giant sign plastered with a picture of the aborted remains of an eight-week-old fetus. She's looking down at her phone and doesn't pay attention to us. An old lady stands next to her, leaning on a walker. A man stands next to her reading out loud from a Bible. No one says anything to us. They don't approach us. It's so hot out that I can see sweat beading on their faces. I feel sorry for them. I don't know why.

I try not to look at the woman's sign, but I can't help it. A blob-like fetus with a bulging forehead and teeny fingers floats in a puddle of blood.

The sign jolts me, even though Annabelle tells me the picture is Photoshopped. But it doesn't make me change my mind.

Bea holds my hand, Annabelle holds the other, and we walk up to the clinic together.

We press a bell outside.

A voice comes over the speaker. "Names and ID, please."

The three of us show our driver's licenses to the camera, and we get buzzed in. It's busy inside. Nearly every chair is taken.

I go to the desk and sign in. A woman behind the desk smiles and hands me a clipboard. I take it back to the chair, but my hands are too shaky to write so Bea fills in the form for me while I whisper the answers to her.

The reality of what I'm about to do hits me hard. It took everything I had inside me to make it this far. It's like those marathon runners you see who collapse once they cross the finish line. That's what I feel like. If they make me sit in a room and explain why I want to have an abortion, like I had to do I don't know how many times now, I'll lose it. I'll fall into myself and never come out again.

Annabelle puts her arm around me, and I lean my head on her shoulder.

A woman dressed in scrubs comes out and calls my name. Annabelle and Bea stand up with me. "Can we go with her?" Bea asks.

"I'm sorry, only patients are allowed back. Don't worry. We'll take good care of her, and I'll come out and let you know when she's all done, okay?"

"Hi, Camille. I'm Sarah," she says when I reach her. She pushes open the door, and I follow her down the hall to a changing room with a bunch of lockers in it. "You can leave your top and socks on but take everything else off. Put all your things in one of the lockers and take the key with you." She hands me a paper drape. "Tie this around your waist and have a seat in the chair outside the door, and I'll come and get you."

I take my clothes off as fast as I can, cramming them and my purse in the locker. The key is attached to a plastic coiled bracelet, and I slide it onto my wrist.

A few minutes later Sarah comes back and takes me into a room with an ultrasound machine. I'm going to have to go through the same thing, the doctor explaining what she sees, the turning of the screen toward me.

None of that happens.

Sarah gives me a little cup with ibuprofen for cramps and an antibiotic to prevent infection. She also gives me an Ativan to relax me. She does the ultrasound, but she doesn't make me look at the screen. She doesn't explain what she sees. She leaves me alone.

Sarah takes me into another room. There's an examining table covered with paper and a machine next to it. The doctor comes in. She's wearing a white coat but underneath she's wearing a T-shirt and jeans. Her long gray hair is in a ponytail. She shakes my hand. "Hi, Camille. I'm Dr. Maria." She sits on a rolling stool next to the table. "Do you have any questions for me?"

"Do I have to tell you why I want an abortion?" I ask.

She shakes her head. "Absolutely not. I'm not the reason police; you don't have to justify anything. I understand you're from Texas. If you've come all this way, you've probably thought it all through, and you know what you want to do. It's not up to me to change your mind.

"I don't want you to worry. The entire procedure is very straightforward and will only take a few minutes."

She has me lie back on the table and put my feet up on the metal stirrups. I'm wearing the socks my mom gave me for Christmas. They have pictures of a girl riding a unicorn. RUNNING THE WORLD AND STUFF is knit on the cuffs.

"Cute socks," the doctor says.

I hear Sarah and the doctor talking, gathering up the things they need. I see the bright lights overhead and hear the creak of the table.

Dr. Maria inserts something in me. I feel a pressure in my stomach followed by a pain that feels like the worst period cramps I've ever had. But the pain only lasts a few seconds. My paper drape rustles, and I feel the doctor's hands as she helps me put my legs down.

"You're all done now, Camille."

I nod.

"Take your time getting up," the nurse says. "You might feel a little woozy, okay?"

I start to cry.

I try to hold it back, but I can't. I don't know why I'm crying. I'm relieved that it's over, that I'm not pregnant anymore.

I cannot stop crying.

Sarah takes my hand. Dr. Maria hands me a tissue and takes my other hand. And they don't say anything; they don't leave me. They just wait.

"I'm . . . I'm sorry," I say when I feel a little calmer.

"Take a deep breath and let it out," the doctor says, her voice full of kindness. "Do you have someone with you? Someone to drive you home?"

"My best friends," I say, knowing it's true. Annabelle and Bea are my best friends, and I know I'll keep them forever, like that waitress said. I put my hand up to blow my nose, and the bracelet slides down my arm, the charms clanking—the Texas flag, the bluebonnet, the western boot, the cactus, and the mockingbird.

Sarah touches it. "Pretty," she says.

"My friends have the same one."

"The girls waiting for you?"

I nod.

"We used to do friendship bracelets when I was little," she says. "I still have them all. In a jewelry box at home."

Sarah takes me across the hall to another room. A group of women are sitting in reclining chairs with heat pads on their stomachs. No one is saying anything. One woman is crying quietly. Sarah settles me into a chair, places a heat pad on my stomach, and gets me a drink of water.

I sit back, closing my eyes. Five minutes. That's all it took. Annabelle, Bea, and I have been gone for days. We've spent all our money. We've been to Alamo, Progeso, Nuevo Progreso, the Texas Panhandle . . . all this way, all this money, for a five-minute procedure.

Sarah returns and escorts the crying woman out of the room. A girl about fourteen years old takes her place. She looks at me; her eyes are exhausted. I wonder how far she traveled. How she got pregnant and what she feels now. But I don't ask her. I don't say anything. I only smile and then look away.

After a half hour, Sarah gives me a bag filled with condoms, a box of emergency contraception, and a booklet about the different kinds of birth control. I get dressed and go to the bathroom. Some clots of blood come out when I pee but not too much. I put the pad the nurse gave me in my underwear and wash my hands and splash water on my face. I pull a brush through my hair and put it into a messy bun. I take a breath and glance in the mirror. I look older. My eyes are different—red from crying, for sure, but wiser maybe. I look like I've been through a battle and lived to talk about it.

The pain pills the clinic gave me make me feel weightless and calm. I spread my arms and legs out on the bed at the motel in a giant X and pull them back in again and again, like I'm making a snow angel. That desperate feeling that's been sitting on my chest since closing night of *Hamlet* is gone. This road trip, the abortion, there are bigger things in my world now, and I think I might be able to handle them.

I fall asleep again, and when I wake up, Annabelle and Bea are gone. I check my phone. Bea texted to say they're getting dinner.

My phone dings with another text.

Léo: *I'm back in France. I don't know if you want to hear from me anymore, but I want to say that*

> *Willow was fabulous but it wasn't what I hoped for because you were not there.*

Me: *I do want to hear from you. I always will.*

Léo: *Will you come to France?*

Me: *Will you hold my hand?*

I watch the bubbles move across the screen.

Léo: *If you hold mine.*

The next morning we leave for Texas. I drive home the last half of the journey. It's nighttime and from the passenger seat, Annabelle sleeps, her head against the window, her knees pulled up against her chest. It's dark, and there aren't many cars on the highway. I pass a Greyhound bus, its passengers silhouetted in the tinted windows. I think about that Simon & Garfunkel song that my parents love, the one about the couple on the bus eating Mrs. Wagner's pies, searching for an America they can believe in. I pass by an RV pulling a car behind it, and I imagine a retired husband and wife selling everything, packing up only the things that can fit in that RV, and heading out into the world, completely untethered to any kind of responsibility. Maybe it's like childhood when your world is bordered by your neighborhood, where Halloween, Christmas, and your birthday is how you measured a year. When climbing a tree or standing up on skates for the first time felt like magic. Where monsters were imaginary and you knew your parents would catch you if you fell.

I drive and drive until Buzzi's headlights shine on a road sign welcoming us home to Johnson Creek in Texas, the Lone Star State.

THIRTY

I'm home, but no one is there. I put all my things away, sorting my laundry in the hamper and folding my empty backpack onto my closet shelf, like it's any other day. I dust my room. I change my sheets.

I carry my laundry downstairs. The step still squeaks, the shag-pile rug is still there, and the pictures remain in the same line. It all looks different to me, though, like I'm noticing things from a different me. That out-of-style rug is comfortable between my toes; the squeaky step reminds me of my dad; and those pictures of Grandma make my heart crack a little.

I imagine my senior picture in that empty space. In my junior year picture, I look out at the photographer with that fake picture smile and shining eyes. I don't remember what I was thinking about then.

I wonder if I'll look different in my senior picture—if my smile will be real, my eyes focused and sure. When things change inside, do we change on the outside?

I take my laundry downstairs and start the washing machine, and then I go back upstairs into the kitchen. The dust on my mom's pots makes me pause. It makes my heart hurt to see them like that. I don't like the dust bunny trapped in the balloon whisk. I take her stuff down and lay it out on the kitchen island. I fill the sink with hot sudsy water and dunk each piece, scrubbing years of dust and kitchen gunk off. I dry them and hang them back up, all but the whisk and a bowl. I look for my mom's baking notebook in the bookshelf, and I turn the pages until I find the recipe for cherry cupcakes with Swiss buttercream frosting written out in my mom's careful handwriting. I get out flour, eggs, milk, cherry flavoring, sugar. I follow each step carefully, mixing the wet ingredients, combining the dry.

"What are you doing?" My mom stands in the kitchen doorway. She's in her bank teller uniform, a blue polo shirt and khaki pants, her purse over her shoulder and keys in hand.

"Making cherry cupcakes. I wanted to take them to the Globe tomorrow."

I pick up her red spatula, the fancy one perfect for folding batter. I start to mix, purposely doing it the wrong way.

She puts her things on the kitchen stool. "Careful," she says. "You don't want to overwork your batter. You want to fold, not stir."

I push the bowl to her. "Can you show me?"

She looks at the bowl for a second, and I don't know what is going through her head. Maybe she feels like Annabelle does, like she isn't good enough; or maybe she's embarrassed to try again, that she's lost her skills. Or maybe she feels like I felt, like it isn't worth it to try again.

I shouldn't have pushed her. I reach for the bowl. "It's okay, Mom—"

She grabs the bowl. "Now listen closely," she interrupts. She picks up the spatula. "You fold by cutting the spatula down the center and bringing one side of the batter over to the other. Turn the bowl and repeat, gently, until the batter comes together. And when that happens, put the spatula down and don't touch it again, okay? Otherwise you'll develop the gluten in the flour and your cupcakes will be tough."

I watch Mom work the spatula, her movements sure and practiced.

"Will you teach me to make macarons?" I ask.

"Macarons are really hard because they are pure technique, but if you keep practicing your skills, I think you'll be up to the challenge." She finishes folding and puts the bowl down. "There." The batter is smooth, the sides of the bowl perfectly scraped clean.

"Use the disher to portion out the mix; otherwise the cakes will bake unevenly. You don't want one burned and one raw." She watches me scoop the batter into each paper liner. "Careful you don't overfill."

"I didn't go to Willow, Mom," I say, releasing the mechanism and dropping a perfectly round scoop into the pan.

"What do you mean? Where were you all of last week?"

I put the disher down. I look at my mom. She's watching me carefully, not zooming around the kitchen doing little tasks or bossing me around like she normally would.

I'm not embarrassed anymore. I'm not ashamed.

"Mom. I have something to tell you."

Author's Note

In 1990, in the small window of time when a woman's right to choose in the United States was a given, I sat staring at my young female doctor as she gently told me I was pregnant. We discussed the choices—I could continue the pregnancy or not. If I chose an abortion, I could make an appointment on my way out of the clinic. I decided right away to have an abortion. I told my ex-boyfriend what I wanted to do, and he gave me half of the two-hundred-and-fifty-dollar fee. There were no protestors in front of my doctor's office on the day of my abortion. The procedure took five minutes, and I was out the door in an hour and back to my life within days. No regrets.

I was a woman in my twenties, living two thousand miles away from my family, and I owned my own business. I was capable. I was independent. But in addition to relief, I felt shame and embarrassment. I told only a few people I could trust. I worried that people would look at me differently if they knew. I worried they would think I was stupid, careless, slutty, irresponsible, selfish. I was terrified people would find out, especially my clients. My face flaming with guilt, I lied about why I had to take a few days off.

I still feel a small bite of shame. It follows me to Planned Parenthood, where I work as a volunteer escort. I feel it pricking at me as I stand in front of the clinic, my heart pounding in my chest, as anti-abortion protestors shout horrible things: *You're going to hell. You're a murderer. Your baby will scream as she's being aborted. The worst black genocide is happening right now in that clinic. Mommy, don't kill me.*

Despite our best efforts to shield patients, they can't help but notice the protestors. They are bewildered by random strangers who make them feel worse than they already do. They don't understand why their deeply personal experience has become public.

It isn't fair. None of this is fair.

I chose to write Camille's story to sound an alarm, to show young women what they have to lose, how their bodies are being regulated, and how their rights to decide when and if to have a child are being slowly taken away by laws that shut down clinics, set abortion limits on gestation periods, outlaw rare late-term abortions (usually used to save the mother's life or prevent a baby's suffering), require fetal burial, and on and on. I wanted to talk about how shame is used as a weapon to control women's reproductive rights.

Because abortion restrictions are in constant flux, it was almost impossible to keep up with the changes as I wrote, so I set the time line for Camille's story in 2014, after Texas passed extreme reproductive laws. I based Camille's story on fact, in particular an *Atlantic* piece from June 2014, "The Rise of the DIY Abortion in Texas." The article tells the story of women who travel to the Rio Grande Valley in search of misoprostol, the abortion pill, on the black market.

In the year and a half it took to write and edit *Girls on the Verge*, new abortion laws in the United States have been passed, challenged in the courts, upheld, or overturned. As I write this on March 29, 2018, the Kentucky House, controlled by Republicans, just passed one of the most restrictive abortion laws in history: an eleven-week ban on the common abortion procedure called dilation and evacuation.

Although seven in ten Americans believe that abortion should be legal, women's reproductive freedom is not assured because the political anti-choice movement is strong. There are protestors at nearly every abortion clinic, some of them peaceful, some of them violent. Abortion providers, support staff, and volunteers have been harassed, doxed, and exposed. Clinics have been shot up, bombed, and burned. Doctors and nurses have been murdered. Officer Garrett Swasey, Ke'Arre Stewart, and Jennifer Markovsky were shot and killed in a Colorado Planned Parenthood in 2015; Dr. George Tiller was shot and killed in his church in 2009; Dr. Barnett Slepian was shot and killed in his home in 1998. Since the early 1990s, there have been eleven murders and twenty-six attempted murders.

It's no wonder that women are afraid to talk about their experience. But to break the stigma of abortion, we have to bring it out into the light. Women who are able to share their stories can help put an end to the fear and the shame.

In January 2017, I walked in the Women's Rights March in Chicago alongside my aunt Pam. She is one of the badass feminists who walked in the 1978 March for the Equal Rights Amendment in Washington, DC. As we joined the crush of people on State Street, she looked at me and said, "I can't believe we're still protesting this." I can't believe it, either. How long will we have to fight to live in this world on our own terms?

Talking about my own abortion scares me because I don't

know how people will react. But I'm fifty-one years old now, and I'm tired of ducking my head and pretending it didn't happen. I'm ready to talk about my abortion now. Like Camille, I'm not embarrassed anymore. I'm not ashamed.

The Facts

Roe v. Wade became law in 1973, making abortion legal in the United States. But it remains up to the states to regulate abortion, and many enacted Targeted Regulation of Abortion Providers (TRAP) laws, which create never-ending regulations on clinics and on women. Nonprofits, such as Texas's Jane's Due Process and Lilith Fund and the National Abortion Federation, help women work around these laws, but it can be overwhelming and taxing in an already stressful situation, and women are often forced to travel many miles, sometimes to another state, to reach their nearest provider. Legal organizations, such as the Lawyering Project, the ACLU, and the Center for Reproduction Rights, challenge these laws.

The possible overturning of Roe v. Wade would mean the end to legal abortions in the United States. Women would still have abortions, but they would have to seek illegal and unsafe abortions.

Texas's restrictions on abortion—noted in the epigraph—were struck down in the Supreme Court (Whole Women's Health v. Hellerstedt) in 2016. But the damage was done. Many women's clinics shuttered in the years it took to appeal.

Pregnancy "crisis clinics" have stepped into the void left by shuttered women's health clinics. These sham clinics and mobile units (often parked near legitimate women's clinics) offer free ultrasounds and pregnancy tests. They offer counseling, which is an attempt to persuade women not to have an abortion. They give incorrect information about contraception and abortion. It is often difficult to tell a crisis clinic from a genuine clinic.

Abortion is common. Despite restrictive laws, as of 2017, one in four women in the United States will seek an abortion by age 45. Fifty-six percent of women who seek abortions have a child already. Thirty-four percent are 20 to 24; 12 percent are teens age 15 to 19. Seventy-five percent of women seeking abortions are poor.

Abortion rates are dropping. Due to widespread availability of contraception, data taken between 2010 and 2014 shows a drop in the abortion rate—teens accounted for 46 percent of the drop. Abortion restrictions exist in most states. The Guttmacher Institute, the leading research and policy organization for sexual and reproductive rights in the US and globally, notes that 43 states have gestational limit prohibitions, 20 states prohibit "partial birth" abortions, and 37 states require parental involvement.

Despite all of this, you, like Camille, have options. If you need help or advice on pregnancy, there are resources available to you. For information on abortion in your state, visit guttmacher.org /state-policy/explore/overview-abortion-laws and the sites listed below.

Planned Parenthood, plannedparenthood.org
NARAL Pro-Choice America, prochoiceamerica.org

National Abortion Federation, prochoice.org
The Guttmacher Institute, guttmacher.org
Jane's Due Process, janesdueprocess.org
The National Network of Abortion Funds, abortionfunds.org
The Lilith Fund, lilithfund.org
National Organization for Women, now.org

Acknowledgments

I would like to thank . . .

Christa Desir and Carrie Mesrobian for the Boobie Bungalow, providing insight into boys and virginity, and for so many other things.

Melissa Azarian, Terri King, Katie Mitschelen, Marina Cohen, Sofia Del Carmen-Maisonet, and Ashley Biggs for listening and offering advice. Thank you, Terri, for providing the title.

My editor, Christian Trimmer, for taking a chance on me.

Mark Podesta, Katie Klimowicz, and the Letterettes for the kickass lettering.

My amazing and supportive agent, John M. Cusick, and Folio Literary Management.

Tina Hester and Amanda Bennett at Jane's Due Process for patiently explaining Texas abortion law and parental bypass.

My fellow Planned Parenthood volunteer escorts, especially Betsy Hunt and Marty Zimmerman. You organize us with humor and kindness.

Texans Cecile Richards, former president of Planned Parenthood, and Wendy Davis, former Texas state senator, who continue to work tirelessly for women's right to choose.

Escorts, volunteers, medical and support staff, and patients of women's health clinics who are forced to run the gauntlet every day. Your bravery is inspiring.

And finally a big thank-you goes out to my husband, Mark, and my family, who have always supported my writing dreams.